THE RUTHLESS KNIGHT

JEANA E. MANN

ONE

Nicky

Two women glide across the ballroom, demanding my attention. The first woman, the one in a tight leopard print gown, stops near the champagne fountain. Females like her make my mouth water—giant tits, a tiny waist, and an ass that jiggles with each precarious step on her towering sandals. The sides of her gown are held together by silk laces, revealing a strip of bare flesh from armpit to knee. There's no question that she's naked beneath. She pauses to dip a strawberry into her champagne glass then sucks on the ripe red fruit with lips that are equally juicy.

"Put your tongue back in your mouth." The second woman comes to a stop at my side. Like everyone here, her face is hidden by a mask, but I know who she is. Unfortunately for me, our lives are tangled together for the foreseeable future. The corners of her mouth dip toward the floor. Which is nothing new. She hates me.

"What I do with my tongue is none of your business. I'll put it anywhere I want." My phone vibrates. A glance at the screen makes me groan. Valentina. Again. She's been reaching out for days. I send the call to voicemail and stuff the phone back into my pocket. "If you'll excuse me, I'm going to see if that lovely leopard will let me put my tongue in *her*—for starters."

"Was that Valentina calling?" The mask can't hide the disapproval in my sister-in-law's gaze. Part of me enjoys her irritation. Serves her right for marrying Roman instead of me. "Won't your girlfriend be pissed that you're cheating?"

"She's not my girlfriend." The very thought turns my stomach. I tug down the cuffs beneath my black tuxedo jacket and try to pretend that her insults don't wound my pride, because I deserve her hatred.

"Really?" Rourke's eyebrows arch toward her blonde hairline. "She's the only woman you've ever dated for more than a few weeks. If she looks like a girlfriend and acts like a girlfriend…"

"We aren't dating. We're—business associates." Just standing next to Rourke evokes a sensation similar to rubbing sandpaper over raw skin. The wound left by her rejection never heals. "If you don't like my company, Mrs. Menshikov, then leave."

Rourke lifts her chin in a gesture of pure defiance. Light from the massive crystal chandeliers bounces off the diamond necklace around her slim throat, probably a gift from my richer-than-God adopted brother. "In case you've forgotten, Nicky, this is *my* event. Maybe you're the one who should leave."

"Roman and I were doing this long before you blundered into the picture." In fact, this is where the three of us met for the first time. Here. On this dance floor. The flutter of her pulse above her collarbone causes a knot to tighten in my chest. Every minute in her presence is pure torture because I can never have her. "Without me, there wouldn't be a masquerade ball."

"And what, exactly, did you do?" From behind the lace of her disguise, her blue eyes flash. "Maybe you helped come up with the concept years ago, but I chose tonight's theme, hired the orchestra and performers, interviewed every single employee. I cultivated the guest list. All you did was screw the party planner."

"You know what I think? All this hostility is a lame attempt to repress your intense desire for my massive cock." I chuckle at her annoyed growl. "Don't deny it. We both know you want it." My gaze returns to the luscious leopard slinking toward the terrace. "Now, if you'll excuse me, I'm going on safari."

"Roman wants to see you." When her hand rests on my forearm, her touch burns through the velvet of my jacket. I close my eyes to savor the contact. Tonight, when I'm fucking someone else, I'll draw on this moment, pretending it's her beneath me and not some random stranger.

"Have your tits gotten bigger?" I let my gaze drop to where her breasts peek above the top of her strapless gown. "They're enormous."

"They never recovered from breastfeeding." She tugs up the sides of her gown.

"And how is Satan's baby?"

"That's a terrible way to talk about your nephew." Anger flames in her cheeks. I'm getting to her, but the knowledge does little to heal my broken heart.

"My apologies." Shame intensifies the ache in my chest. What's wrong with me? I give her a stiff bow, preparing to leave.

"Roman's in his study." For the second time, she halts my escape by touching me. I stare at her hand until she drops it to her side.

"Doesn't he ever take a day off?" It's my turn to groan. My workaholic sibling and his wife love to ruin my fun. But not this time. Not tonight. Tonight, I'm going to dance a little, drink too much, and rut like a stag. I'm horny as hell. Being around her and her magic boobs doesn't help. "I'll find him later."

"He said it was urgent." The scent of citrus and honey hovers around her. My blood buzzes like a bee.

"Everything is urgent to him. Just because he used to be a prince and owns half the world doesn't mean everyone should bow at his feet." Beneath my calm façade, resentment simmers in my veins. If I don't get away from her, I'm going to shatter. "Catch you later."

I stride toward the terrace doors where my leopard girl has disappeared. Rourke's gaze weighs heavily on my backside. On impulse, I spin around, hold my hands apart in the approximation of ten inches, lift an eyebrow, and nod. Amusement flickers across her lips. Deep down, she likes me. If I'd been a better man, she'd be mine right now. The truth is I don't deserve her. Never will. With a sigh of resignation, I square my shoulders. The animosity between us is a necessary evil. It's the only way I can save my pride.

On my way past the bar, I grab a bottle of Macallan and two glasses. The orchestra begins a lively waltz. A sea of women in colorful gowns floats over the marble floor, held fast by their partners. I skirt the edge of the orchestra. The musicians, like everyone else at this party, wear masks to conceal their identities. No names. No faces. At the Masquerade de Marquis, celebrities and royalty rub shoulders with everyday people. Invitations are exclusive. And nothing is off limits. A flutter of excitement lifts my spirits. Behind a mask, I can be anyone I want. And tonight, I'm a big game hunter in search of a leopard.

The air on the terrace is fresh and a welcome change from the crowded ballroom. I pause at the top of the steps leading down into the garden to watch the breeze toss the fountain spray. Overhead, stars sprinkle the night sky. From this vantage point, I have a clear view of the torchlit pathways. Performers dressed like fairies and sprites tumble and leap among the foliage and flickering lights. In the distance, the stone tower of a castle rises above the treetops. My leopard is nowhere to be found.

No matter. The night is young, and there are plenty of other women at the ball. After a swig of whiskey straight from the bottle, I weave my way down the path from the manor house to the castle keep. The five-story tower is all that's left of the medieval fortress that used to sit on this site. I withdraw the all-access keycard from the inside pocket of my jacket and swipe it through the electronic reader. The locks on the enormous wooden door click.

My footsteps tap on the flagstones as I wander the labyrinth of corridors until I reach the great hall. Once this room housed knights and kings. The echoes of their chainmail and ancient revelry still reverberate from the rafters. On this April evening, noises of a different kind fill the room. Filthy, decadent, naughty noises. Skin slapping on skin. Moans of ecstasy. The scent of sex hangs in the smoky air. In the dim light, flashes of naked bodies peek out from the shadowy corners.

"Hello, handsome." A woman wraps her fingers around my bicep.

"Hello." When I turn to see who is touching me, I'm met by a svelte dishwater blonde. She's completely nude except for a tiny red thong. Small, firm breasts jut between us. I can't help staring. "And hello to you, too."

"Want to play?" The red plume on her mask soars into the sky, jerking with her head movements.

"Always." Just what the doctor ordered. A pretty girl has always been able to solve my problems—or at least provide a temporary distraction.

"I want you to meet my friends." She threads her fingers through mine, pulling me up a narrow spiral staircase into a small side room.

I blink. It takes a second for my eyes to adjust to the

darkness. Sitting in a high-back leather chair are two women. The brunette in front grinds her ass into the woman seated behind her—my leopard girl. The leopard glides her hands along the brunette's breasts, over her ribs, to slide between her legs. I'm instantly hard. The blonde releases my fingers, leaving me in the center of the room, and kneels between the brunette's open thighs.

"Don't be shy. Come on in." The leopard's voice is husky, sultry. Without ceremony, she dumps the brunette to the side and offers her seat to me. "I'm glad you found us."

Three women. What have I gotten myself into? Heaven, that's what. I shrug out of my tuxedo jacket, throw it aside, then lower myself into the chair. The brunette sits at my feet. The blonde perches on the armrest. And the leopard—she circles to the back of the chair where I can't see her. Once there, she leans down to whisper in my ear. The locks of her platinum wig brush my jaw. "This is your lucky night, big boy."

Don't I know it. The blonde tugs the knot from my bowtie. The leopard unbuttons my shirt before dipping her hand inside to caress my pecs. Her touch is warm and confident, just the way I like. Rourke, the tension with my brother, the fucked-up mess of my life—they're all forgotten as this beauty toys with the hair on my chest.

"What do you like?" The leopard is obviously the leader of this threesome. Confidence drips from her sultry voice. Her fingers strip away my shirt while the other girls kiss each other. "Do you like watching them? Is that your thing? Watching?"

"Yes." The declaration rasps from my dry throat. "I like watching and being watched." I've built an empire on the fantasy of voyeurism. First, with this medieval tower in Sussex. Then with satellite clubs in New York City, Chicago, Los Angeles, and a dozen more locations around the world. Membership to the Devil's Playground is curated, exclusive, and very expensive. If these girls have a keycard to the castle, they've been vetted by my staff.

"We'll do anything you want. Please you any way you desire." The leopard's full lips brush mine. She drags my lower lip between her teeth and tugs until it stings. I hiss in pleasure. "Tell me what you want, handsome."

"I want you on your knees, sucking my cock." I grip the back of her neck, careful not to disturb her wig, tight enough to let her know I prefer to be the dominant one.

A smirk twists one corner of her luscious mouth. "I like a man who knows what he wants." She jerks away from my grasp. In one smooth motion, she twists onto my lap, her back to my chest. The thin fabric of her gown leaves little to the imagination. I can feel the seams of the cloth, the round softness of her bottom, and the heat of her body. The scents of fresh linen and soap cling to her movements. She circles her bottom over my groin. Her movements are slow, controlled, teeming with wantonness.

"I saw you in the ballroom. You're stunning." I run

my hands over her full breasts, enjoying their weight in my palms.

"I saw you, too." She reclines completely. The back of her head rests on my shoulder. This position aligns her face with mine. "I was hoping you'd find me."

Our mouths touch in the briefest of kisses. Her lips are softer than I expected. Hunger builds inside me. I haven't had a good blowjob in forever. Work has kept me too busy. Running multiple businesses, catering to Roman, and commuting between continents leaves little time for anything but sleep.

"Do you belong to the club? I haven't seen you before."

She ignores the question. Her hips make slow, leisurely circles, grinding on my cock. One of her hands smooths up her thigh, over her ribs, to join my hand in cupping a breast. The slow sensual movement creates an ache in my balls.

"No more talking. Just sit back. Let me pleasure you." Words every man loves to hear from a beautiful woman. Her request brings joy to my soul and blood to my dick. Especially when she slides to the floor, opens the fly of my trousers, and frees my straining erection from its prison.

The sight of this beautiful creature between my spread knees is enough to obliterate my bad mood. The tip of her tongue glides over her full bottom lip, drawing my attention to the mole at the left corner. The mask can't hide the dimple in her chin or the golden hue of her skin. Temptation nags my common sense. One tug of the silk bow at the back of her head would drop the barrier between us and show me who she is. I won't do it. First, because it's against the rules of the club, and second, because I don't want to know. It's so much hotter this way, knowing I can fuck her mouth then walk away without hurt feelings. But if she asks for my name, I'll give it to her.

"Magnificent." The unfamiliar, male voice in the shadows reminds me that we're not alone. Club members can spy on any scene at any moment through the numerous peepholes in the castle. Sparks ignite and catch fire in my veins. Nothing turns me on more than the taboo act of being watched.

"You're a big boy." The leopard encircles her thumb and forefinger around the base of my erection and slides them to the crown with the perfect amount of force to elicit a hiss from me. She teases the head with her tongue. Her next words make my heart leap. "I can't wait to have you in my mouth."

My heart kicks against my ribs. I tilt her chin up so I can look into her eyes. I can't tell what color they are, only that they're dark. With the pad of my thumb, I trace the swell of her lips. She's luscious. Tempting. I want to do all sorts of unchivalrous things to her full curves, but she's in control of this scene.

While the blonde and brunette make out, the leopard wraps her lips around my head. I dig my fingers into the arms of the chair at the drag of her teeth over my shaft. She's gentle, practiced, applying the right amount of pressure in the correct places. My crown hits the back of her mouth. The muscles of her throat contract as she swallows. I groan. "You're good. Really good."

I've had lots of blowjobs from lots of women. None of them compare to this. The scope of my world drills down to her and her mouth. Within minutes, I'm coming. She remains between my open knees, her hands resting on my thighs, watching me, waiting. I close my eyes, lean my head back against the chair, and enjoy the flood of endorphins.

A swathe of light cuts across the room as the door opens. "Playtime is over, ladies." The deep voice of my brother ruins my bliss. The two girls stop fondling each other and blink up at Roman. The leopard casts a startled glance over her shoulder.

"It's okay." I raise a hand, bringing everyone in the room to a halt. "He's leaving."

"Everyone out." Roman snatches the brunette's dress from the floor and tosses it toward her. "We have business to take care of."

A bubble of anger swells in my chest, threatening to burst. The leopard slinks back onto her heels, still crouching between my legs. With an exasperated sigh, I shove my cock into my pants and lift the zipper. She gives me a resigned smile. "Too bad. I was just getting warmed up."

"Don't make me ask again." Roman's eyes glitter from behind his plain black mask. The girls scramble for their clothes at the command in his voice. He's the picture of darkness. Black tuxedo. Unruly black hair. Black shirt and tie. His heart isn't visible, but I know from experience that it's black, too. Like a lump of coal at midnight.

"You're a real cockblocker," I snap to Roman. The leopard rises to her feet. I grab her wrist, halting her exit. "You and me. Later. Where can I meet you to finish this?"

"I'll find you." She kisses the tip of her index finger then presses it to my lips. I watch her backside swing on the way to the door. Halfway there, she casts a glance over her shoulder. Her demeanor reeks of satisfaction and mischief. I'm intrigued. For the first time in too long, hope blossoms inside me. Maybe this is the woman to fill the gaping wound in my chest left by Rourke.

"Get dressed." Roman snatches my jacket from the chair and shoves it into my chest.

"This had better be good." I shove my arms into the Armani suit and stuff my bowtie into the breast pocket.

Roman pivots on a heel, striding toward the door, confident that I'll follow. And I do. Not because I want to, but because I swore an oath to protect and serve the heirs to the Menshikov dynasty. I'm his knight, and he's my sovereign. We walk in silence down the corridor to a hidden door, take the winding spiral staircase to the storage vault, and use the secret tunnel connecting to the manor house for our escape. When we're back in his study, I head straight for the bar.

"I know I've told you this before, but you really piss me off sometimes," I confide as I pour two fingers of his best scotch into a tumbler.

"Get over it." Roman strips away his mask, dropping it on his desk. He scrubs both hands through his hair. "God, I hate that thing."

"You used to love it." A hint of accusation lingers in my statement. "You used to crave the mystery and intrigue of this night."

"People change, Nicky. I'm married. I've got a son and a wife. Once you fall in love, you'll learn there's more to life than drinking and fucking."

"Hmph. I'll have to take your word on that." I drop into the nearest chair and toss a leg over the arm. With a tug on the strings of my mask, the disguise falls into my lap.

Roman shoves back in his chair, making the springs creak, and stares down his nose at me like the regal prince he once was. Before his parents were assassinated. Before the exile. His features smooth into blankness. "You're always so angry. Why is that? Go ahead. Get it off your chest."

A lifetime of resentment simmers in my veins, dying for a chance to escape. "You boss me around like you're my dad. Or maybe it's because…" My voice dies away. I bite the inside of my cheek to keep the truth from tumbling out. *Because you have everything, and I have nothing. Because I sacrificed my freedom to keep you safe.* The words stay stuck in my head, but I feel them in my heart. My gaze drifts to the framed portrait of Milada, his daughter, sitting on the coffee table in front of us. Damn him. Seeing her safe and happy makes everything I've done worthwhile. I swallow past the knot in my throat, unwilling to open this Pandora's box.

Suddenly, I'm very tired and feeling much older than my thirty-two years. I swirl the whiskey around the tumbler, watching the amber liquid churn. I can't continue talking about the wounds of my past. Not when the scars are finally beginning to scab over. "You didn't interrupt the best blowjob of my life to discuss my feelings. What's the emergency?"

"I need you to do a job for me."

"And this job can't wait until tomorrow morning?" Resignation washes away the intensity of emotion. This is my life. I'm trapped in a world of lies, subterfuge, and servitude.

"Tomorrow morning you'll be hungover, and I need you at the top of your game for this." He shakes his glass of whiskey. The ice tinkles against the walls of the tumbler. The gesture annoys me. Everything he does scrapes against my nerves.

"Maybe I don't want to work for you anymore." I force a smile. "Maybe I'm done with your bullshit jobs."

"Really? Are we going to do this dance again? The one where you pretend you're not going to do it, and I pretend you're serious?" A muscle twitches in his cheek, a sure sign of his frustration with me. "Let's cut through the crap and get to the payoff. I'll double your fee on this one."

"It's not about the money."

"Since when?" His reply demonstrates his low

opinion of my past behavior. Can I blame him? He has every reason to doubt my motives.

"Since Don McElroy." We fall silent, contemplating the recent struggle to free Roman's homeland from the Machiavellian schemes of the former Vice President of the United States. "Do I need to remind you that *I'm* the one who found him for you? Not one of your henchmen. *Me.* And I asked for nothing. In fact, I was wounded in the process." My goal isn't to brag, but to defend my tattered honor. "Where were you during the search for McElroy?" I tap a finger to my lips, pretending to think. "Oh, that's right. You were holed up in your Manhattan fortress with your new wife, making babies and counting your money. Meanwhile, I was out there doing your dirty work. I'm the one who brought him back. Not you. Not your minions. Me." With each word, my anger climbs. "I'm the one who has the bullet wound to prove it."

"You were shot in the ass. A wound that required nothing more than some antiseptic and a Band-Aid."

His constant refusal to recognize my efforts is more than I can take. He has no idea the sacrifice I made to keep our loved ones safe. It's too much. "Fuck this. And fuck you. I'm out of here." I stab my arms into my tuxedo jacket then reach into my pants pocket for my diamond cufflinks. They aren't there. Come to think of it, my Rolex and keycard are also missing. They must have fallen out in the castle. "Damn it."

Roman opens the humidor on his desk, withdraws two cigars, and hands one to me. The glower on his face softens. Beneath his intimidating exterior, he is—and always has been—a decent guy. A fact I'll never admit to him. "Don't leave, Nicky. I apologize. Sit and we'll talk this through. Without your help, none of us would be here to have this conversation today. I'm truly grateful."

"Too little. Too late." My phone buzzes with an incoming text. Valentina. She always did have impeccable timing. Until now, I didn't believe my luck could get any worse. I drain the last drops of liquor from my glass and set it on the coffee table. "I'm out of here."

The door bangs shut on my heels. I fume as I retrace my steps to the keep. An uneasy thought begins to form. What if the leopard girl and her friends stole my stuff? I'm not usually an easy mark, having lived with questionable characters my entire life. However, this wouldn't be the first time a pretty face and a hard dick have led to my downfall.

What a terrible night. With my mask in place, I close the door, intending to head for the garage where my precious Porsche awaits. It'll be a cold day in hell before I tell Roman about my stuff. He'd laugh his ass off. I'll deal with this myself. And now, Valentina has summoned me. A request I can't refuse. My thoughts jumble together—images of Rourke's disapproval, the leopard girl's luscious curves…

A flash of platinum catches my gaze. It's her, rushing toward the circular staircase. I break into a jog and catch up to her just as she's about to flee out the door.

TWO

Calliope

My heart pounds in my ears. It's been a successful night. Cash will be ecstatic. We've stolen a crap ton of jewelry and money from these elitist fools, and it was surprisingly easy. The power of big tits and a willing mouth will never cease to amaze me. I let my accomplices, Athena and my sister Jagger, do most of the seduction. Except for one. Mr. Big Dick. The guy with the sculpted features and rock-hard ass had been mine—a welcome perk of the job. Too bad he had to leave so soon. His massive cock had tasted even better than it looked.

I race down the hidden staircase as fast as my high heels allow. At the next landing, I hop from the left foot to the right, unfastening the straps of the gold sandals to bare my feet. The narrow stone steps are cold on my naked soles, but I'm faster this way. My footsteps slap with each stride. My lungs sting from the effort. I'm out of shape. Too many donuts and too much TV have dwindled my stamina. Adrenalin, however, fuels my escape. One more flight, and I'm home free.

This is the only thing I love about my job. The danger. The heady rush of success after a big score. Except this isn't one of my usual con jobs. My future, my freedom, and *my life* depend on making a clean getaway. I bobble on the next step, slamming into the wall. A nail snags on my dress and rips the leopard print fabric, baring a strip of skin near my belly button. The borrowed gown hugs every inch of my full figure, but the tear allows me to draw a deeper breath. I increase my pace, skipping over the last two steps.

The exit door is exactly where Cash said it would be. We spent hours going over blueprints of the historic house, plotting my escape. So far, everything has gone as planned. My two co-conspirators reach the door before I do. Athena and Jagger pause on the threshold. Elaborate feathered masks cover their eyes, like everyone else at this midnight masquerade ball. I've never been a team player, but Cash insisted on Athena's presence to keep an eye on me.

"Go," I snap when the women bottleneck the hallway.

"Wait." Panic blooms in Jagger's eyes. "My phone. I left it upstairs."

"Leave it." Athena gives her a ruthless shove. My hackles rise. No one shoves my little sister.

"My life is inside that phone. If someone finds it, they'll know who I am." Jag's normally low voice escalates to an anxious soprano. "I've got to go back."

"What the ever-loving fuck?" I groan. This is why I wanted her to stay home. She's too inexperienced, but she had begged, and I gave in, like I always do.

"I know. I'm sorry." Her oval face scrunches into a frown. "You guys were rushing me."

"No one's going anywhere." Athena's cold features have turned icier, something I hadn't thought possible. No wonder Cash chose the pseudonym for her. *The huntress.* She's a tall, willowy blonde with Amazonian legs, perky tits, and sociopathic tendencies. "I should never have let you bring her. She's dead weight. When Cash finds out about this, he's going to be pissed."

Jagger had been a last-minute addition to the team. I never wanted this kind of life for her, but she's a natural-born thief. And Roman Menshikov's Masquerade de Marquis seemed like a fun way to break her in to a big-league project. With the masks hiding our faces, risk of exposure is limited. And I hated to leave her back at the hotel alone where she could get into mischief. At least this way, I know where she is.

"Fuck Cash." The last person I care about is my ex-boyfriend who is now banging the Amazon. He forced me to do this job when he knows how much I want to quit and live a life free from his control.

"Please." The last shreds of Jagger's calm dissipate. Beneath the heavy makeup and designer gown, she's nothing but an eager twenty-two-year-old. Her fear elicits sympathy inside my cold, dead heart. My first big job had been scary, as well. I'm such a bad sister.

"We can't jeopardize this assignment because you're

too stupid to keep track of your belongings." Athena lifts the hem of her gown and draws a tiny pistol from the holster strapped to her thigh. She levels the barrel at Jag's forehead. "I'm sorry."

"Wait." My heart leaps into my throat. I wedge myself between the two women. If we're caught, we'll all go to prison—providing Cash doesn't kill me first. And he would. He's never been known for his mercy. "Let's all calm down. We can work through this. It's not a big deal. No one has to get hurt."

"You'd better talk fast then, because I'm not going to jail over a stupid phone." Athena lowers the pistol, but she doesn't move.

"I'll go back and get the phone. You two get the car. Pull around to the service entrance. I'll meet you there." Before anyone can protest, I shove my sandals into Jag's hands and sprint up the steps, two at a time.

The hallway is dark and quiet. A shiver rolls up my spine. How many centuries of scandal have occurred beneath these coffered ceilings? I try not to dwell on the shadowy corners, the haunting coats of armor, or the austere portraits staring down at me. Instead, I concentrate on retracing my steps and avoiding detection.

I spy the glitter case of Jagger's phone on the floor beneath the framed Picasso—or where it used to be. The oil painting was small, about the size of a postcard, and oh-so beautiful. The temptation had proved too much. After Mr. Big Dick left, I stripped the canvas from the frame and gave it to Athena for safe keeping. Cash will be thrilled to acquire an expensive original work of art like that. Maybe thrilled enough to release me from our bargain. With the phone in my hand, I race to the secret stairs. At the door, two strong hands grip my biceps. The door swings shut, cornering me in the narrow passageway with a very tall, very angry man.

"Gotcha." The deep voice rumbles through me. It's Mr. Big Dick. His lips are close to my ear—close enough to feel the hot puff of his breath against my neck. Shivers of fear and desire spawn gooseflesh on my arms. A muscular chest presses against my backside. The buttons of his shirt bite into my spine.

"Let go." I wriggle, but there's no escaping his tight grasp. My pulse doubles. *No. No. No.* This can't be happening. Not when I'm so close to earning back my freedom.

He spins me around, trapping me against the wall. Behind the holes in his mask, his eyes are turbulent pools of gray, thick-lashed, and angry. "I don't think so."

The dimple in his chin accentuates a clean, sharp jawline. *Swoon.* An hour ago, I had his glorious cock in my mouth and enjoyed every minute of it. I glance away to keep my traitorous body from reacting to his blatant sexuality. ""I was looking for you. I got turned around. This place is so confusing. Do you want to go somewhere and finish what we started?"

"Liar, liar, pants on fire." A smirk curls the corners of his sensual mouth. "I'm the best liar ever. So, I know what I'm talking about."

He's about twelve inches taller than I and a good

deal heavier. I shove against him with my hips and hands, testing his strength. He answers by trapping my wrists above my head. Easily. Like I'm an unruly child. His right palm presses against my stomach and brushes the belly ring bared by the tear in the dress. The spread of his fingers over my abdomen does strange things to the space between my thighs.

"Now, where are my things?" His gaze sweeps down my body. The form-fitting gown leaves little to the imagination. My traitorous nipples jut against the stretchy spandex. He smooths a hand over my ribs, probing the cleavage between my breasts. A pulse of attraction makes my insides clench.

"I'm telling you—I don't know what you're talking about."

"We'll see." He snatches the phone from my hand. "Did you steal this, too?"

"No. It belongs to my friend. She dropped it. I was going to return it to her."

"More lies." His hand moves lower, finds the split in the dress at my hip, and travels up the inside of my thigh. When his thumb brushes my pubic hair, I hiss—partly from the unexpected tingle between my legs, partly from indignation.

"Mm…no panties? How daring." He blows out a heavy breath. "If only we hadn't been interrupted earlier. Such a shame. I would really like to know what it feels like to have your legs wrapped around me. But, no matter." He clears his throat like he's gathering his composure and continues his leisurely exploration of my body until he's satisfied. "Where are my things?"

My fingers curl into fists, but I'm helpless to move. He's too big, too heavy, too strong. "Please. You don't understand. If I'm not downstairs in two minutes—"

His elegant fingers wrap around my throat. "No, *you* don't understand. You've fucked with the wrong person."

"Are you going to call the police?" The only thing more frightening than Cash's wrath is the coldness in Mr. Big Dick's eyes.

"That's not how we handle things around here." His gaze dips to my mouth. The tip of his tongue sweeps along his lower lip in anticipation of *something*—something I know I won't like. His mischievous smirk returns. "You took something from me, and now, I'm going to take something from you."

His mouth crushes against mine, brutal and dominating. My knees weaken. I'm not sure if it's from the tongue plundering my mouth or the strong fingers wrapped around my windpipe. He tastes like whiskey, smells like expensive cologne and cigars, and touches me like he knows his way around a woman. All the things I've longed for in a man. I kiss him back, ignoring the alarm bells sounding in my head. I've always been fucked up that way—attracted to the wrong kind of guys, the kind who dominate and take me for granted. I don't care. I'm screwed no matter what I do. If I don't meet the others at the car, Cash will hunt me down and kill me. If I let this masked marauder take me hostage, I'm probably already dead.

The situation seems hopeless, but I've never been one to give up. I'll go down fighting to my last breath. I sigh and lean into him, opening my mouth wider. It's not the first time I've used my body to get what I need. He releases my hands to cup a breast. I grab on to his lapels and remove his car keys from his pocket in the process.

Athena appears behind my captor. Before I can speak, she lifts a nearby vase and whacks him in the back of the head. His knees buckle. He slumps to the floor. I watch in open-mouthed shock.

"Come on." She grabs my elbow and drags me down the narrow stairs.

"Are you insane?" Our whispers echo in the quiet.

"Hurry up." At the next landing, she pushes in front of me. "Stupid bitches can't follow directions."

We shoot through the service door. I grab the skirt of my gown and follow her through the damp grass to our extraction point. Jagger is waiting in the shadows. Suddenly, the pieces of tonight's puzzle fall into place. No matter what we do, this is going to end badly for Jag and me, and I just can't have that. When Athena turns her attention toward Jagger, I punch her in the jaw with all of my weight behind my fist. Her head snaps to the left. She drops to the ground.

"Who's the bitch now?" I ask her unconscious figure, still seething with fury over her actions tonight. Violence has never been a part of my routine, but I'm not afraid of defending myself or my loved ones when necessary.

“Wow, sis. That was impressive.” Jag stands over Athena, peering down at her. “Nice hook.”

“Help me.” I prod Jag into action. Together, we drag Athena into the bushes. “Come on.”

“What about the stuff?” Jag nods toward the duffle of stolen items.

“Leave it.” Taking Jag’s arm, I drag her toward the garage. Athena moans, slowly fading back to consciousness. We only have seconds to get out of this mess.

Inside the garage, motion lights snap on as we walk past rows of gleaming, expensive vehicles. I press the buttons on Mr. Big Dick’s key fob until one of the cars chirps. A few minutes later, Jag and I are roaring down the road in Mr. Big Dick’s Porsche. Athena will never catch up to us in this sexy machine. Cash can go fuck himself. I’ve been waiting for a chance to escape his control for a decade.

THREE

Nicky

Sixteen hours later, I disembark Valentina's private plane on the tarmac of a Colombian airport. Thanks to last night's trio of beauties, I have a knot on the back of my head, a king-sized headache, and a wounded ego. I should be angry, but I'm not. Instead, I'm impressed. Breaching Roman's security deserves the utmost respect. According to him, the women relieved a number of guests from their priceless jewels. I endure his angry rant on my ride from the airport to this warehouse.

Heat shimmers above the asphalt in the narrow alley. I'm in the bad part of Cartagena, the part smart men avoid. A trickle of sweat crawls between my shoulder blades. It's so damn humid here. I hate this city. Not because of the heat. Because of the memories and the obligations and the disgust I feel for myself every time I visit. While I wait for someone to open the warehouse door, I use my handkerchief to wipe the perspiration from my forehead. Behind me, the taxi driver stomps the accelerator to the floor, launching his cab forward with a squeal of tires.

"Enter." The intercom speaker distorts the gruff Russian voice. A buzzer sounds, the locks click, and the door swings open. My heart gallops in my chest. I pause long enough to get a grip on my nerves then cross the threshold.

The strong stench of dust, mold, motor oil, and exhaust assaults my nostrils. I try to breathe through my mouth, ignoring the taste of those things on my tongue. Through the dimness, the shapes of cars—expensive ones—begin to take form. Lamborghinis, Maseratis, Maybachs, Bugattis. All stolen. All about to be chopped or sold or shipped to foreign allies as gifts. I skirt the perimeter of the vehicles and climb the rusty iron stairs to the second-floor office overlooking the warehouse floor.

"Ah, the whore is back." Yuri Sokolov is a big guy, barrel-chested but fit. "Come in, whore. Sit."

Although I'd like to punch his ugly face, I manage to maintain a neutral expression. "Is she here?" Hopefully, after today, my bargain with Valentina will come to an end. I slide into the leather club chair next to Viktor, his henchman. I want to get this over as quickly as possible and get back to living my life.

"You know, I was just telling Vik that we haven't seen you here in forever. We've missed your smiling face." As he speaks, he pours three shots of vodka into short glasses. "Perhaps Valentina has tired of you. Maybe she's replaced you with someone younger. Someone with a bigger dick."

I accept the vodka, hoping it will take the edge off my hangover from last night. Vik watches me through heavy-lidded eyes. Tension thickens the air among the three of us. "I don't know about that. My dick's pretty big."

"If my wife is not happy, I am not happy." He reclaims his seat behind the desk and smooths a hand over his more-salt-than-pepper hair. "And you will answer to me for that."

Despite the air conditioning, my dress shirt clings to my skin. "I'm here because you can't get it up anymore." I shift in the chair, cross a leg over my knee, and try to pretend my life isn't in danger of ending. Fear has a distinctive odor. I've smelled it on my enemies more than once. Maybe Vik and Yuri smell it now—on me. "If you were fulfilling your husbandly duties, we wouldn't be having this conversation."

"Is that what she tells you? My mistress would say otherwise." He lifts the vodka to his thick lips, downs the shot in one gulp, and takes a minute to study my face. "You should be more like Roman. He would never become whore to another man's wife." His gaze crawls over me, searching for cracks in my calm façade, eager to regain the upper hand in our uneasy relationship. Well, he doesn't need to worry. I've offered my soul on a silver platter to his wife. He stops staring long enough to light a cigar, puff on the end, and send clouds of thick, white smoke into the stale air. "Roman is arrogant. I like his testicles."

I choke back a chuckle at his stilted English. "Balls." Yuri frowns at my correction. "You mean balls." When his scowl deepens, I wave a hand. "Never mind. Anyway. While I'm here, maybe you can help me out with something."

His laughter booms through the room. Even Vik cracks a smile. "A favor? You come here after you fuck my wife and your brother slaughters my men, destroys my business, and steals my weapons? To ask a *favor*? Perhaps you are the one with enormous testicles." The smile drops from his face. "Either you are crazy or stupid. I don't know which. Tell me one reason why I shouldn't end your life right now."

At my elbow, Vik nudges aside the lapel of his suit coat to reveal the leather gun holster strapped beneath his arm. My bowels turn watery. Coming here was a bad idea. I should never have made a bargain with Valentina, but I did it anyway. For Rourke. Because sacrificing my self-respect and body meant she'd be safe from Don McElroy. Now that Don is safely imprisoned, I want my freedom back.

"You need me." The answer leaps off my tongue. I've always done my best work under pressure. The kind of pressure exerted by Yuri Sokolov turns coal into diamonds or dust. I prefer to become a diamond.

"Without me, you'll have no one to deal with Roman. Without Roman, you have no guns. And without guns—well, you get the picture."

"Sad but true." Yuri exchanges glances with Vik. The portly man relaxes into his chair. I swallow down the fear clogged in my throat. Yuri jerks his head toward the door. "Perhaps we can be of use to each other. Come."

The three of us clatter down the metal staircase. I follow Yuri between sky-high stacks of barrels to the back of the warehouse. Vik walks behind me. Two men dressed in disposable coveralls greet us. The scene behind them escalates my anxiety. Sheets of plastic cover the walls and concrete floor. Seated on a chair in the center of the room is a man about my age. Zip ties tether his ankles to the legs of the chair. His hands are bound behind him. Terror shines in his eyes. The room smells of blood, fear, and death. Things I've scented too many times during my life.

"I apologize for the interruption. Please continue." Yuri twirls a finger in the air, encouraging his minions to resume their work. The dispassionate gleam in his eyes is almost as disturbing as the implements of torture lined up on the adjacent workbench.

"What did he do?" My voice is calm and confident. Inside, I'm none of those things.

"He lied to me, Nicky. To my face. And now he has to pay the price." The big man places a placating hand on the shoulder of the prisoner. "Do not fret, comrade. It will be over soon enough."

I glance at my watch. "Valentina's not here, and I have another appointment. Maybe I should come back."

"Your favor—what is it?" A single bead of perspiration rolls down his temple and hangs on the point of his chin.

The faces of the men turn to me. I lick my lips to ease the dryness, stalling. On the plane ride here, I rehearsed my speech a dozen times, but nothing prepared me for this. After a deep breath, I plunge ahead. "I'm looking for three women—beautiful ones—working as a team with sophisticated knowledge of security systems. They stole jewelry and artwork, and I want it back."

Vik sucks in a shocked breath. Yuri's head snaps back like I've struck him. The droplet of sweat falls from his face and lands on the shiny patent leather toe of his shoe. Even the captive ceases to struggle against his bonds. He draws a white handkerchief from his pocket and drags the cloth over his forehead. "I have heard of them. They work for Cash Delacorte."

"Where can I find this guy?" The chances of reclaiming the stolen items are small, but I need vindication.

He closes his eyes, rubbing two fingers over the furrow between his eyebrows. When he opens them, a gleam of challenge flickers in his dark irises. "Cash is a friend and business associate. My answer is no."

I shrug and head toward the door. "Roman said you were losing your edge. But if you're afraid..."

In unison, three pistols point at my head. Roman had

also said that coming here was a suicide mission. I lift my hands in the air. Fear weakens my knees. I always knew my final breath would be drawn while staring down the wrong end of a gun. Now that the moment is here, I'm swamped with regrets. I should have been a better person, told fewer lies, stayed away from married women, started a family. As much as I don't want to die in a scummy Colombian warehouse, I doubt anyone will miss me.

"Say the word, boss, and I'll take him out." The cold steel of Vik's gun barrel presses against my temple. "I've always hated this fucker." He pushes harder until my head tilts to the side from the force. "On your knees, Nicky."

"Are you sure? This is a custom Italian suit." Desperation forces me to stall. I grasp for any reason to distract or delay the inevitable.

"What is this?" A feminine voice with a heavy Colombian accent draws Vik's attention. He lowers the pistol. The overhead light reflects off her shiny, dark hair as she moves to Yuri's side. Five men in matching black suits hover in her shadow.

"Valentina, my love." Displeasure flattens Yuri's lips. "You should have called. We're in the middle of personal business."

"I don't need to call. This is *my* business, Yuri. You work for me, or have you forgotten?" The fabric of her pink jumpsuit clings to her large breasts, narrow waist, and wide hips. She rakes long fingernails over his cheek in a wicked caress. "Tell me now. What is going on? Don't make me ask again."

I ease away from Vik. The movement draws Valentina's attention. Her brown eyes study my face. I give her a casual grin. "Hello, Valentina."

"Nikolay? You made it. What took you so long?" She pushes past Yuri, ignoring the captive tied to the chair. When the tips of her tan sandals touch my toes, she stares up into my eyes. "Have you missed me?"

"No." I return her stare with equal temerity. The scent of jasmine floats around her. From my stance, I can see straight down her bosom. "The only reason I'm here is to tell you that I'm done."

"Don't be like that, baby." Her fingers trail down the lapels of my suit then back up again. Although her demeanor is friendly and flirtatious, I know better. Death and destruction cling to her high heels. Even Yuri keeps a respectful distance. "You've been a bad boy."

"I suppose that's a matter of perspective." Just standing next to her makes me want to hurl.

With a sweep of her hand, she tosses her sleek hair over her shoulder. "When I call you, I expect you to be on my doorstep within twenty-four hours. I was about to send Vik to get you."

"I wish you'd keep your whores out of my warehouse," Yuri sputters.

She lifts a hand to shut him up. His mouth snaps closed. An obedient pit bull on a tight leash. "We had a bargain. I provided you with the man who threatened to kill your beloved sister-in-law, and you agreed to be my whore."

"That was three years ago. It's time to renegotiate." A pact with Valentina Sokolov is akin to a deal with the devil.

"You seem to respond well to threats. Maybe you'd be more accommodating if I brought your beloved niece here to spend time with me. What is her name? Milada?" The bottom drops out of my stomach at the mention of Milada's name. Valentina's gaze locks with mine. "How old is she now?"

"Fifteen." The lump in my throat intensifies.

"Such a tender age for girls. She's at a boarding school in New York, right? And such an excellent student. Good grades, pretty, a champion equestrienne. Is she a virgin, too? A beauty like her would go for big dollars on my auction block."

The fire in my veins turns to ice at the threat. "You wouldn't dare."

"Try me." A cold smirk twists her bright red lips. "In fact, my men have eyes on her right now." She digs out her phone from her purse, presses redial, and holds up the screen to me. It's a live video of Milada in her school uniform, walking through the school campus. One of her men wearing dark sunglasses walks a few paces to her left while another holds the phone. My guts shrivel in a way I'd never thought possible.

"We might be able to work something out." I refuse to add more disappointments to the infinite list of ways I've failed Milada. My life already belongs to Valentina.

Despair hangs on my shoulders, heavy and relentless. At this rate, I'll never be free of her.

"Yuri, kindly tell your men to point their weapons elsewhere." Valentina's gaze locks with mine. "And, Nicky, you come with me. We can discuss the specifics of our new agreement over dinner. Have you eaten yet? I have reservations."

The last thing I want to do is eat. Being around her nauseates me, but if I refuse, she'll make good on her threats against Milada. I won't let that happen.

After a shared bottle of wine and a plate of empanadas at an upscale restaurant, Valentina places her hand on my knee. My skin crawls at the touch of her blood red nails on my leg. "Now, who are these women you spoke to Yuri about?"

"You were listening?" I don't know why I'm surprised. There isn't an inch of Yuri's business that she doesn't know about. He might be the leader, but she's the true mastermind behind his enterprise.

"Of course, darling. Yuri is useful but stupid. How else can I keep him out of trouble?" The sharp edges of her claws rake up and down the inside of my thigh, making the spicy food curdle in my stomach. Everyone knows her marriage to the Russian mobster was one of convenience. Their union promoted her from a Colombian smuggler to an international powerhouse and tripled their wealth. Together, they're formidable. "I've heard of these women. In fact, one of them is of particular interest to me."

"Is that so?" I straighten, allowing her hand to climb a little higher on my leg.

"Yes. She's a voluptuous woman, big ass, even bigger tits." She cups her hands in front of her to indicate a large bosom. Her eyes narrow into dark, predatory slits. "This woman stole from me. If you could bring her to me, I'll end our bargain. Forever."

FOUR

Calliope

For the past two nights, the same guy has sat in the same corner booth of the bar, drinking Macallan highballs and watching my every move. A stranger. Not one of the many regulars who circulate through the doors of this Ohio sports bar. His elegant grace, the expensive suit, the perfect hair—they're incongruous with the football jerseys and baseball caps of the other patrons. My gaze snags on his for the hundredth time tonight. The collision forces the breath from my lungs. Brutal like a punch to the gut. He shifts back in his seat, cloaking his face in shadows.

"He's hot, isn't he?" Edna edges up to the bar and stares at the mystery man. "If you like that type."

"What's wrong with his type?" I ask, a little too brusquely.

"Nothing. If you like a perfect, arrogant, pretty man. Me? I prefer a beer-drinking, sports-loving teddy bear like my Tim." She rests an elbow on the counter, her chin on her fist, and watches him.

"For goodness sake, stop staring. He's going to think we're talking about him."

"We *are* talking about him." Challenge eddies in her eyes made larger by her red plastic-framed spectacles.

Ignoring her, I perform the rote task of pouring drinks for the other waitress while a sliver of suspicion tightens in my chest. It's been three months since I slipped away in Mr. Big Dick's Porsche. When I reached London, I sold the car to a sleazy dealer and bought a one-way ticket to the most obscure place I could find. What if Cash sent this guy? As quickly as the thought occurs, I push it away. Impossible. No one could ever trace me here. I was careful to cover my tracks. I've got a fake ID and the lecherous bar owner pays me cash to avoid taxes.

I'm so focused on not looking at the guy in the corner that I accidentally trip over the rubber mat at my feet, stumble into the wall, and almost upset a stack of clean shot glasses. "Crap."

"You should go talk to him." Edna steadies the glasses before they crash to the tile floor. "You know you want to."

"No. I don't." I fill two mugs with Guinness from the tap, set them on her tray, and ignore the questions in her voice.

"It's just—" She falls silent as Lloyd, the other bartender, hovers at her elbow to grab coasters and cocktail napkins.

"Can you close up?" he asks. "I've got somewhere to be."

"Sure," I reply.

The instant he leaves, Edna leans over the counter to reclaim my attention. Sincerity softens her features. "Guys hit on you all the time, but I've never seen you leave with one. Why is that? You're still young. You're pretty. Do you prefer women? It's okay if you do. No one here will judge you for it. In fact, I know a really nice girl from—"

"Not your business." I arch an eyebrow but tolerate her concern because she's my only friend.

Edna ignores the warning in my tone and continues. "It's not. And I really don't care, except—except you've been a raging bitch for the past month, and we're all tired of tiptoeing around you." The confession tumbles out of her mouth in a rush, like it's been hovering on the tip of her tongue and she can no longer hold it back. "You're always angry. Always guarded. What's going on with you?" When I don't answer, she keeps going, even though my back is to her. "You never hang out with any of us. You don't talk about your personal life. It's like you don't exist outside of this bar." Her brow furrows in an otherwise unlined face. "It's weird. That's all I'm saying."

"Better get back to work." Using my knee, I close the storage cabinet beneath the counter and pivot to face her. Unlike the other employees, my glare doesn't dampen her determination. "Those beers won't serve themselves, and I want to close up at a decent hour tonight."

Lloyd bumps my backside, causing vodka to splash over the glass I'm holding and onto my shoes. I scowl. "Watch it, Lloyd."

"Sorry." He keeps moving, like he's afraid I might jump down his throat. The pained scrunch of his forehead reinforces Edna's accusations. The realization saddens me.

"Just go home, would you? I can finish up." My tone is gruffer than necessary. Being a jerk gets easier with each passing day. I hardly remember the sweet, sunny girl I used to be, the one who died on my fifteenth birthday. It's safer this way. If I'm prickly, no one will dare to breach the fortress I've built around myself. I place two shots of peppermint schnapps on the counter and lift an eyebrow at Edna. "Are you done blowing me shit? Or do you need something else?"

A frown tugs down the corners of her wide mouth. "I'm worried about you."

"Don't be." Her confession brings a lump to my throat. Aside from her, no one cares about me. Not one, single, solitary person in this world gives two shits about my welfare. I shove the self-pity into the deepest, darkest pit of my soul to fester alongside the rest of my useless emotions. I brace both arms against the counter. "Let me save you some time. I'm not worth the trouble."

"Hey." Her small hand covers mine for a brief moment before I shrink from the contact. No one has dared to touch me in a very long time. I curl my fingers into fists at my side. The softness in her expression is enough to bring the sting of tears to my eyes. I want to break down and confess the darkness lurking in my soul, to lighten the load I've been carrying for sixteen years, but I can't. If it were just me, I'd unburden my conscience in a second. Others, however, depend upon my silence. So, I keep the shield intact around my secrets and glower at the man in the corner. She's not fooled by my expression. "Whatever happened to you—whatever you're hiding—just know that you can always talk to me."

"Thanks." I duck my head, pretending to check the cooler beneath the bar, but it's really to fight back the burn of emotion in my throat. How many times have I longed to confide in someone? To lighten the burden on my back? I want to, but I can't. No one will ever know the unholy secrets that I carry. "After you deliver those drinks, you can head home."

"Are you sure?" She glances around the bar. Everyone has left but the enigmatic guy in the corner booth and her customers. Her reluctance wars with her desire to get home to three kids and a doting husband. "I don't like you being here alone so late at night."

"I can take care of myself." To cement my sincerity, I grab the rope suspended from the brass bell next to the cash register and ring it. "Last call. Drink up. Time to go home."

"All right." Edna shrugs and bustles to deliver her drinks.

Edna's college kids gulp down their beers then leave. She clocks out, leaving me alone with the guy in the booth. I watch him from the corner of my eye as I move through the closing routine. Normally, I would let Edna stay while I shut down, but I don't want her around on the odd chance that this guy is here for me.

In the corner, the handsome man sips from his glass, his stare vigilant. After a few minutes, he stands and stalks toward me. I ignore him, watching his progress from beneath my lashes. To my relief, he brushes past. On the way, he drops a hundred-dollar bill into my tip jar. A few feet from the door, he stops and comes back. My heart skips a beat.

"What's your name?" His voice is deep and rich, his accent more international than American and vaguely familiar.

"Who's asking?" I stare up into a face sculpted by the gods. Lord have mercy, he's got a dimpled chin and square jaw and the most beautiful gray eyes I've ever seen. Mr. Big Dick had gray eyes, too. The random memory is troubling.

His gaze crawls over my breasts, lingering on my bare belly before climbing back to my face. "Does it matter?"

"No. Not at all." My hands shake as I drop dirty glasses into the sanitizing solution. Why did I let Edna leave? "Thanks for the tip. It was very generous. Now, if you'll excuse me, I need to close up."

He ignores my statement, claiming the nearest bar stool. The gracefulness in his movements reminds me of a panther circling prey. The hairs at the nape of my neck lift. "Aren't you afraid to be here alone so late at night? This side of the Cleveland isn't known for its safety."

"I can handle myself."

"May I keep you company?" His clasped hands rest on the polished surface of the bar. His fingernails are manicured. A bold ruby and platinum ring circles the third finger of his right hand, and matching cufflinks peek from beneath his coat sleeves. "This is my last night in town, and I really don't want to sit in my hotel room alone. Do you mind?" A sincere smile curves his lips. "Please?"

Every cell of my brain warns against this man. He's too polished, too perfect. Meanwhile, my body thrills at the subtle scent of his cologne, the masculine angles of his jaw, and the strength in those long, elegant fingers. Edna was right. It has been too long since I've been with a man. So, I ignore the warning bells in my head and smile back at him. "Okay. Sure. Would you like another drink?"

"Only if you'll have one with me." Sin and the promise of seduction drip from his words. A pulse of attraction flutters between my legs.

I pour two shots of Macallan and nudge one toward him. He takes the glass between index finger and thumb. We clink the shots together in an impromptu toast. The expensive whiskey warms my insides as it slides down my throat. "You're paying for these."

"Of course." Our gazes hold for the length of a heartbeat. It's been a long time since any man caught my attention. This guy—there's so much more to him than good looks. He's got manners, charisma, and primal heat lurking beneath his custom suit.

"So, where are you from?" To regain my composure, I concentrate on wiping down the bar.

"Many places, but mostly New York. You?"

"I was born in Indiana, but I've lived all over." Talking about myself always makes me uncomfortable. Thinking about my childhood reminds me of the misery it contained. I rapidly deflect the question. "Are you in town for business or pleasure?"

"Business. But I've never been against a little pleasure." Sin and mischief curl the corners of his lips into a smirk. "How do you feel about it?"

"About what?" My gaze locks on his mouth, the sweep of his tongue over his bottom lip, the neatly trimmed beard and moustache covering the sharp angles of his jaw and chin. Heat races up my neck when I realize I'm staring. I drop my attention to the bar, pretending to scrub a nonexistent spot from the polished wood.

"About mixing business with pleasure." The way his tongue rolls over the word *pleasure*, drawing it out, makes my nipples tingle. I bet he can do wicked, nasty things with that tongue. Make a girl scream in toe-curling, sheet-clenching ecstasy.

"In my experience, pleasure is a foreign concept to the majority of men. At least where women are concerned." For a brief moment, a flash of my former self takes over. My flirtatious tone matches his. I lean forward, bracing on an elbow, giving him an eyeful of my cleavage. His pupils dilate when I trail a finger along the curve of my collarbone.

"Then you'll be thrilled to know that I'm an exception to that rule. You see, pleasure *is* my business."

"So, you're a pimp?" I bite my lower lip to hide a smile when his eyebrows shoot up.

"Not at all. I make fantasies come true for the richest of the rich. Whatever their hearts desire." His voice drops lower, a dangerous caress of promises and temptation. "I can make *your* fantasies come true."

I bet you can. The answer circulates through my consciousness. For a brief moment, I'm caught up in the possibilities for the future. This man, naked and writhing in my bed. Me on my knees, bent over this counter. Both of us panting and sweating on the pool table across from the bar. Then I remember who I am. "Another time. Another life. But not tonight, hotshot."

"Pity." His stare weighs on my backside as I walk to the end of the bar. "I'll get out of your hair. How about one more for the road?" He lifts his shot glass into the air.

"Sure." I avoid his gaze as I refill his glass and mine.

"To pleasure." We clink glasses once more. The liquor traces down my throat. Within seconds, a pleasant numbness spreads through my chest and into my fingertips. He withdraws a crisp twenty from his wallet and drops it on the counter in front of me. "Enjoy your evening."

Streetlamps cast golden pools of light on the sidewalks. In the distance, the skyscrapers of the city illuminate the night sky. Aside from the occasional barking dog or police siren, my neighborhood is dark and quiet. I tug the lapels of my jacket tighter around my waist to fight away the November chill, resisting the urge to glance over my shoulder—again. Soft footsteps thud on the pavement behind me. He's back there. I feel his gaze on me. Those bedroom eyes are crawling over my backside, the same way they did at the bar. He's been following me for the last block. Maybe longer. Always at a distance, but close enough to keep me in sight.

Don't panic. I repeat the words beneath my breath. The entrance of my apartment building looms in sight. My strides lengthen, but my legs feel heavy. I take the concrete steps two at a time to the security door. I try to slide the key into the lock, but my hands are shaking too much. They slip through my grasp and land with a clatter at my feet. "Damn it."

"Allow me." His voice is nearer than I anticipated. Almost at my ear. The hairs on the back of my neck lift. How did he get so close so quickly? He bends down, retrieves the keys, and straightens to meet my gaze.

"It's fine. I've got it." I reach out a hand.

He ignores the gesture. The ends of his scarf flutter in the breeze. He's taller than I am, has the broad shoulders and slim hips of a man who takes pride in his body.

A pulse of attraction hits me between the legs. Despite his beauty, his politeness, his aura of composure, there's something sharp and brutal in the depths of his eyes. In another life, I would've taken him up to my apartment for a nightcap. But not tonight. Not when all my senses scream for me to run.

"I insist." He uses my keys to open the building door and gestures me inside. He crosses the threshold behind me. I try to calm my racing heart.

"Are you following me?" I wait for him to return my keys.

Instead of answering, he heads toward the elevator with my keys in his hand. The doors open immediately. I hesitate. Am I being silly? Paranoid? I took painstaking measures to protect myself from Cash's henchmen. There's no way Cash sent this man. He presses the button for the fourth floor—*my* floor—and the doors swoosh shut, trapping me inside with him.

"It's late to be walking around this side of the city alone. I wanted to make sure you made it home okay." He rolls his lips together, like he's choosing his words. "I thought you might change your mind about the *pleasure*."

"No. I didn't change my mind." The scents of leather, spice, and musk hover above the usual building smells of floor polish and disinfectant. We stand shoulder-to-shoulder, staring at the beige metal doors. Men like him don't visit this building. Goosebumps crawl along my forearms. My intuition is seldom wrong. This guy is dangerous.

"You have my keys." For the second time, I extend a hand. A cold sweat breaks out on my upper lip. When was the last time I ate? Breakfast? I lean against the wall, fighting the urge to close my eyes and sleep because the heaviness in my limbs is overpowering.

The elevator chimes as we pass the second floor. He drops the keys into my open palm. "You didn't think I was going to keep them, did you?" His tone is light, teasing, almost playful.

"No. Of course not." I clench my fingers around the plastic key ring, noticing how the playfulness doesn't reach his eyes. I've seen eyes like his before—angry, arrogant, predatory. Once he disembarks, I'll make an excuse, ride the elevator back to the lobby and take the stairs to my floor. Except I'm so drained of energy that I can barely keep my chin from hitting my chest.

"Are you feeling okay?" His stare bores into me.

"Just a little dizzy. It's nothing." But it is *something*. The sweating, the dizziness, the trembling in my limbs.

The doors open. "After you." He sweeps a hand toward the hallway, blocking the control panel and emergency call button. My panic escalates. I resist the urge to rub my sweaty palms on my jeans. Mostly because I'm too tired. Each step is like slogging through wet cement. His fingers wrap around my elbow, saving me from a collision with the wall. "Easy. Let me help you into your apartment."

"I'm fine. Seriously. Thank you." I smile, forcing my expression to remain relaxed and open. "My roommate is home. I don't want to wake him."

"We both know that's not true." A hint of amusement curls the corners of his mouth. "You don't have a roommate." The briefest flash of mischief ignites then gutters from his expression. When I don't move, the doors start to close. He shoves a hand between them. They bounce open again. His voice lowers. "Go ahead."

"You're not a businessman. Who are you, really?" My voice cracks on the words.

"Why don't we go to your apartment? We can discuss it there."

"I don't think so." I scan the hallway for options. Two of the four apartments on this floor are vacant, and my neighbor is out of town. If I scream, will anyone hear me above the squabbling married couple on the next floor? My gaze lands on the fire alarm directly across from the elevator. An option I'm not above using.

"Don't be stupid, Calliope Jones."

My heart pings against my ribs as my real name falls from his lips, a name I haven't used in months. At the end of the hall, the emergency door opens, and the biggest man I've ever seen steps from the shadows.

"Who sent you?" All I can hear is the rush of blood through my ears. This can't be happening. "Was it Cash?"

"Like I said, we can discuss this in your apartment." My companion jerks his chin toward my door.

"I don't know anything." I back up until my rear end hits the wall.

Confusion flickers across his face. He shakes his head, moving closer until I feel the heat from his body.

His breath puffs against the shell of my ear. "We can sort that out—*in your apartment*. Let's go."

My knees quake as we walk toward my apartment. His hand grips my hip, guiding me to the door. I don't know what disturbs me more—my predicament or the perverse attraction pulsing between my legs.

Inside my apartment, he takes a seat on the sofa and smooths a hand down the length of his silver paisley tie. An expensive tie with a gleaming diamond-studded tie bar. His opposite arm stretches along the back of the couch. The smart lines of his pristine navy suit contrast with my shabby living room. I stand in front of him, weaving with exhaustion. His gaze crawls over the modest décor, the pile of books on the floor, the laundry basket of unfolded clothes in the hall. When his attention reaches my face, I feel a rush of heat race up my neck. "Judge much?" I ask.

Something like a smirk curls the corners of his mouth. It's the first sign of humanity that he's shown. The tip of his tongue drags over his lower lip in a slow, sensual sweep. "Do you have anything to drink, Ms. Jones?"

"What do you mean?" My befuddled brain is unable to process his presence or his request.

"I'd like a drink. Wouldn't you, Viktor?" The big guy hovers in front of the door. Annoyed by my confusion, the businessman's left eyebrow shoots toward the ceiling. "Alcohol? Liquor?" On the back of the sofa, his fingers drum an impatient tattoo.

"No. I don't drink at home."

"Not at all?"

"No."

"Never?" His tone rises incredulously. "Not ever?"

"No. Not at all. Not ever."

"I don't believe you."

"Look for yourself." I sweep a hand toward the kitchen.

"Curious." A sigh of disappointment gusts through his pursed lips. "Well then, let's just get to it, shall we?" He nods to the chair across from him. "Have a seat."

I slide into the dilapidated recliner, grateful to get off my wobbling knees, too afraid to challenge his authority. He shifts forward, resting his forearms on his knees and clasping his hands between them. The adjustment puts us at eye level. I want to look away, but I can't. I'm mesmerized by the facets of emotion, turbulence, and fire in his gray irises. Fear bubbles in my chest. This must be the way a rabbit feels when staring into the eyes of a lion. Trapped. Resigned. Terrified.

"I'm in a bit of a predicament, Calliope." His words are fluid, the elegant speech of a wealthy man. "And I hope you can help me out."

"Okay. Sure. If I can." I rub my sweaty palms over my thighs then curl my fingers into fists. Maybe he'll leave if I'm compliant.

"You see, Calliope, a few months ago, someone robbed me at the Masquerade de Marquis." My breath catches. He's Mr. Big Dick. The sexy guy from the ball. He notes my reaction before continuing. "I mentioned this robbery to a friend of mine. Maybe you know her.

Maybe you don't. Doesn't matter. Anyway, she was very interested when I told her what happened. It seems that this girl who robbed me did something to piss off my friend." His index fingers steeple and point to me. "That's where you come in."

A thousand regrets roll through my head because this is how I'm going to die. I should have been nicer to people. I should have tried bungee jumping. I should have told Jagger how much I love her. We'd parted in a rush. I sent her on her way with the key to my safe deposit box and directions to make a new life for herself. Now, she'll never know how much I regret abandoning her, because this beautiful man is probably going to tie a cement block around my ankles and drop me into the Cuyahoga River. Sparks of determination catch fire in my belly. Jagger would never let a man get the better of her. Nor will I. My spine straightens. "Who are you?"

"Sir Nikolay Reznik Tarnovsky, at your service. But, please call me Nicky." He's still wearing the same smirk, like a cat with a belly full of cream. At least one of us is having a good time.

I shiver and back away to hide the tight points of my nipples pressing against my shirt. Because even though he's here to harm me, I'm attracted to his aura of danger.

"When I saw you last night, I thought for sure I'd made a mistake. You don't look at all like the girl who sucked me off at the masquerade."

"That's because you've got the wrong person." The

heat in my blood cools. I'm equal parts aroused and terrified. "I'm nobody."

"It's not *who* you are as much as *what* you are." He shakes his head, rubbing the back of his neck, and peers up at me through his long, dark eyelashes. The sofa groans as he leans back. "To be honest, I don't really care what you've done or why. I just know that I promised my friend to bring you back. And no one goes back on a promise to her. Not even me."

I swallow through the dryness in my throat. "Please. I don't know this woman. I'll do anything. Just let me go."

"Really? Anything?" Mischief flashes through his eyes. "I'm intrigued." He rests an ankle on top of his opposite knee and spreads both arms across the back of the sofa. His casual, relaxed demeanor stirs my temper. He bobs his head. "Go on."

"I didn't mean…" But I did. My voice trails into nothingness. Would I sacrifice my body for my freedom? Hell, yeah. It wouldn't be the first time I slept with a guy to get out of an unfortunate predicament. A poor girl learns to work with what God gave her. And, lucky for me, God gave me big tits and a round ass.

An electronic buzz breaks his unnerving stare. He withdraws a phone from the breast pocket of his jacket and frowns at the screen. "As much as I really like this game, I'm on a deadline." After typing a return message, he pockets the phone and stands. He extends a hand, palm up. "Let's go."

In the back of my head, a clock ticks down the last

minutes of my life. I can't leave with this man. I back up until I hit the table behind me. I feel blindly beneath the table for the gun taped to the underside. The holster is empty.

He frowns, marring the perfect beauty of his face. "If you're looking for your pistol, it's right here." He pats the waistband of his trousers. "We can do this the easy way or the hard way. Your choice." His voice is smooth and melodious, almost soothing. He wiggles his fingers, gesturing for me to come closer.

"I'll take the hard way." In a desperate burst of adrenalin, I grab the lamp and swing it at his head. He ducks. The lampshade misses his face by inches. Although the swing didn't connect, it's enough to throw him off balance. I leap over the back of the sofa, intending to sprint for the bedroom. He grabs my ankle, following me to the floor.

We grapple in the middle of the room. Our grunts and heavy breathing rip through the quiet. If I can just get to my room, I can lock the door and go out the fire escape. He anticipates my next move, overpowering me with his size. I land on my ass in the middle of the hard floor. He straddles my hips, pinning my wrists to the floor above my head. He's much stronger than he looks, and I'm helpless. The last of my strength ebbs away. Darkness descends, blotting out the ceiling and his angry expression.

FIVE

Calliope

The only sound in the room is rhythmic breathing—mine. My eyelids are too heavy to open. A deep, dreamless sleep wraps clutching fingers around my consciousness. An overwhelming sense of urgency lurks beneath the fog in my brain. I need to wake up, but I don't know why. Luxurious linens and a soft mattress cradle my body. In the far distance, I hear the crackle of a fireplace. The scent of cigar smoke hangs in the air.

Danger. The word echoes through my head in a seductive whisper. *Wake up. Now.* I struggle to the surface, slogging upward through the thick soup in my brain. I groan, lift to a sitting position, and shake the fog away.

"Welcome back." The deep, male voice escalates my anxiety. I know that voice. "You've been out for quite a while."

"Where am I?" Nothing makes sense. Not the twinkling lights of skyscrapers outside the wall of windows. Not the unfamiliar modern furnishings of the bedroom. And definitely not the man sitting in the leather club chair at the foot of the bed.

"Manhattan. In my penthouse." That face—so brutal —so cold. I remember that face.

"New York City?" Fragments of memories tug at the corners of my mind. I struggle to fit the snippets into a coherent picture. The handsome man, his footsteps on the sidewalk behind me, the ride up to my apartment in the elevator… "How long have I been asleep?"

"It's seven o'clock in the evening." He pauses to draw from his cigar. "I'm sure you have questions. I'll try to answer them if I can." The smoke curls in tendrils around his head. "Why don't you take a minute to collect yourself? Hop in the shower. There are clean clothes hanging on the back of the door. I hope you don't mind, but I took the liberty of packing a few things for you."

"I don't understand." Every fiber in my body screams for me to run, but it's all I can do to drag my legs over the edge of the bed. My bare feet dangle above the thick white carpet.

"Easy. No need to rush." In a slow, graceful motion, he rises from the chair to pour a glass of water from a crystal pitcher on the dresser. He hands it to me. "Here."

I cup the glass between my palms, staring at the cool water. "You drugged me." It's the only explanation for my memory loss, the sluggishness of my limbs, the lingering fog in my brain. "How?"

"I slipped it into your shot glass at the bar when you turned your back. It's a new thing. A gel that coats the glass, virtually tasteless and undetectable. And it's time released, meant to hit you about the time you reached your apartment."

Stupid, stupid girl. I stare at the water.

Amusement twists his lips. "Don't worry. It's just water. I promise." To prove his point, he takes a sip from my glass before handing it back to me. "I overestimated the dosage and gave you a little too much. My apologies. The effects should wear off in a few hours. Aside from a little dizziness, you'll be fine."

Sparks of fury ignite in my belly. The bastard. I drain the glass and hold it out for a refill. The only sound in the room is the glugging of liquid into the glass and the banging of my heart against my ribs. This is bad. So much worse than I could have imagined.

"Are you going to rape me?" An icepick of fear stabs my chest. It wouldn't be the first time a man abused me, but it's not something I care to have repeated.

He takes his time before answering. "As tempting as I find you, the answer is no." His steel gaze crawls from my toes, up my bare legs, to my face. Making me aware that I'm only wearing a T-shirt and panties. "I consider myself a connoisseur of all things carnal and forbidden. Role play, bondage, dominance—those are just a few of my favorites. Rape, however, isn't—and never has been —a part of my agenda."

"But drugging and kidnapping an innocent woman is okay? I'm glad you have boundaries."

"I'd hardly call you innocent. As for my boundaries, let's call them flexible." He shifts back in the chair, resting an ankle on the opposite knee, to continue his cold stare. "You can blame yourself for this situation. If my friend wants you, it's because you've done something to deserve it."

The entitlement in his tone raises my defenses. "I haven't done anything to anyone." With a huge amount of effort, I force sweetness into my words. "Please. Just let me go. No one has to know. I'll never say anything to anyone."

"We both know that's not true." He stands, smoothing a hand down his ridiculous necktie. Matching yellow diamond cufflinks sparkle in the glow of the overhead light. "Take a shower. Get dressed. Meet me in the dining room. I'm sure you're hungry." My stomach growls in agreement. "We can discuss what happens next."

The possibilities are too bleak for consideration. An icy shower washes away the last of the cobwebs in my brain. My aching muscles yearn for a soak in the adjacent jetted tub, but this is no time for indulgence. I need all my faculties if I'm going to escape this maniac's clutches.

Once I'm dressed, I make a quick search of the room. He took the water pitcher with him. The furnishings are simple, modern, composed of warm woods and sleek metals. The dresser drawers are empty. Not even a clothes hanger in the closet. And that window. It stretches from the thick carpeting to the coffered ceiling, providing a view from at least thirty stories above the street.

The bedroom door is unlocked. With my hair hanging in damp ringlets, I wander down the hall. Despite my anxiety, I'm acutely aware of the priceless photographs, original oil paintings, and decadent sculptures on display. The minimalist décor provides the perfect backdrop for the art. Although I hate this man, I have to admire his taste.

At the end of the hall, I contemplate my options. The penthouse is open concept with soaring ceilings and lots of windows. To my left is the dining room. The long table is set for six. An elaborate arrangement of white flowers adorns the center. To my right, the front door is within sight. A mere dozen yards away. With a little luck, I could sprint there.

As if reading my thoughts, the hulking man from my apartment corridor steps into view. He blocks my escape with his wide torso. One of his thick eyebrows lifts. Sweeping a hand in front of him, he gestures toward the dining room.

"You're early. Fantastic." Nicky appears from the living room. "I was just about to pour myself a scotch. Would you care to join me?"

"No." What's wrong with this man? His pleasant demeanor confuses me. Am I a prisoner or a guest? I'm not sure.

"Ah, well, suit yourself." With the air of a man

accustomed to nice things, he pours amber liquid from a crystal decanter into a matching glass. "How was your shower? Feeling better?"

"I've been drugged and kidnapped. How do you think I feel?"

After an exasperated sigh, he scans my damp hair, clean face, and the dress he'd chosen from my closet. "Pissed. Confused. Anxious." He taps his lower lip with an index finger. "But not frightened. No, you're not scared at all, and I find that fascinating."

"Your hospitality is a little weird."

"I'm a criminal. Not a barbarian."

"Dinner is ready." A matronly woman in a chef's uniform steps out of the kitchen. She wipes her hands on her white apron as she speaks. "If you and your guest would like to be seated, we'll begin."

"Excellent. Thank you, Marta." Nicky gestures toward the table. "After you, Calliope." He pulls out a chair for me then takes a seat at the head of the table to my left. Viktor sits on my right. Nicky smiles. "Such an interesting name, Calliope. Tell me, was your mother fond of carnival rides? Personally, I've always loved a good freak show."

I gape at him. In the space of twenty-four hours, I've been transported into an alternate universe, one filled with unbelievable art, Michelin-star-worthy cuisine, and the sexiest man I've ever seen.

When I don't reply, he waves a hand. "No matter. It's a lovely name. I like it."

"I'm so relieved." I don't try to curb the sarcasm in my tone.

A butler arrives at my elbow, complete with white gloves and black suit. "Tonight, the first course will be scallops and winter truffle tartare tossed with sourdough croutons. The main course is sesame crusted ahi tuna, seared, and paired with a white wine reduction and jasmine risotto. For dessert, Madame Marta has prepared apple tartlets with fresh cream and lavender."

"It sounds delicious, Cornelius. Thank you." Nicky snaps his napkin onto his lap. The butler uncorks a bottle of wine and proceeds to fill our glasses. "Where are my manners? You haven't been formally introduced. Calliope, this is Viktor, my business associate." The hulking man nods, his gaze chilly.

I wave away the wine. "What happens next?"

"So much for small talk. All right, then. You'll spend the night here, and tomorrow we'll deliver you to your new home."

"And then what happens?"

The pause following my question is long enough to make my stomach lurch. He drops his fork to his plate. "I don't know. It's beyond the scope of my duties. I only procure things. What people do with them after—" He lifts one shoulder in an elegant shrug. "Not my business."

Now I'm no longer a person. I'm a *thing*, to be bought and sold and traded. Although the food looks delicious, I can't eat. Soft classical music floats in the background at odds with the total terror churning in my chest. "At the very least, I deserve to know where I'm going. I deserve a fighting chance."

"There is no chance," Nicky replies flatly. "I'm sorry, Calliope, but it's true. Where you're going is the end of the line. No one comes back."

My heart sinks. I've done a lot of appalling things to a lot of people over the years. Most of them deserved it. All of them had been wealthy beyond measure. In the beginning, it hadn't seemed so terrible, to steal from the rich. Those people had everything while I had next to nothing. After a while, I did it more for the thrill than greed. Until Cash Delacorte came along. He forced me to do his dirty work, ripping off his rivals and keeping the money for himself.

"So, this is my going away party?" The remark is meant to be glib, but no one smiles. "I wish you'd told me. I would've worn something more appropriate."

The rest of the meal passes in a blur. Tension thickens the air. Viktor and Nicky speak to each other like they're strangers. My host sits at the head of the table, but he glares at Viktor like he's uncomfortable with his presence. The food is good, and despite my anxiety, I manage to clean my plate. Then I'm back in my room, staring at the locked door, hating myself for allowing this to happen.

The minutes drag into hours. As I sit on the edge of the bed, I think about Jagger, the father who left us, and my deceased mom. Will Jag bury me next to her? Or will I just be tossed into a ditch like garbage, never to be heard from again? A knot forms in my throat. Maybe this is what I deserve. I've never believed in karma until now.

When the door opens, I jump to my feet. In that split second, my mind is made up. I won't make this easy. If I'm going to die anyway, I might as well go out fighting. Nicky enters the room, closes the door, and leans back on it. We stare at each other for a long minute before he gestures for me to sit.

"I won't go." My voice trembles on the declaration. "You'll have to kill me."

"Nope. Not an option. She wants you alive—to make you suffer." His words intensify the fear gnawing at my insides.

I wrack my memories for a woman that I've wronged. There have been so many marks during my career. All men.

He takes a seat in the chair and leans forward to rest his elbows on his knees. "Where can I find the man you work for? Cash Delacorte?"

"I don't work for him anymore." I shrug, unwilling to let him see my growing fear. "The job at the masquerade was my last."

"You disappeared without a trace. And believe me, I searched for you."

"Obviously, you're not very good at it or you would have found me before now." I stare back at him while my brain rapidly searches for options of escape. He never locked the door behind him. Is Vik outside? Can I even leave the building once I'm out of the apartment?

"But I did find you, didn't I, Calliope?" Cruelty

highlights his flawless features—his straight nose, high cheekbones, and those sculpted lips.

I glance away to regain control of my thoughts. "If I'm going to die, do I get a last request?"

He studies my face with stormy gray eyes. "Maybe. If it's within the realm of my resources. What would you like?"

"Some ice cream?" I end the question with my best, innocent lilt.

"Sure." He stands and turns to leave. "Is chocolate okay?"

"Perfect." I wrap my fingers around the lamp on the nightstand. When he's two steps from the door, I yank the cord from outlet. A primal growl rips from my throat. I charge at him, lamp raised high over my head, preparing for battle.

For someone so tall, he's fast. Before I can bring the lamp down on his head, he whirls, and we tumble to the floor. His heavy body lies on top of me. Tears of frustration and anger leak from the corners of my eyes. I buck my hips, twisting and turning. His knee wedges between my legs. He pins my wrists above my head. I'm immobilized on the soft carpet, able to feel every dip and swell of his body, the strength of his muscles, and the hardness of his thighs.

"Stop. Struggling." The steel in his tone escalates my fear. We're breathless and panting. He holds my wrists with one hand, reaches into his pocket with the other. My hair flops into my eyes as I twist beneath him.

He grunts when my knee grazes his groin. "Careful. Don't do anything you're going to regret."

The sick thing? I'm equal parts aroused and furious. I'd love to rip off his shirt and drag my nails down his back, to feel that monster cock inside me. I know it's twisted beyond measure, but I can't help myself. Instead, I let out a frustrated growl. "It's too late for that."

Zip ties tighten around my wrists then my ankles. No matter how hard I fight, he keeps overpowering me. Triumph glows on his face. He smirks, his full lips inches from mine. "I know."

SIX

Nicky

Three months. Three long, agonizing months to find this woman. There's no way in hell I'm letting her escape. Her dedication to anonymity has been impressive, but that part of her life ends with me. She's been a worthy adversary in every respect. In another time, another life, I would've fucked this woman within in an inch of her life. Brought her pleasure like she's never known. My sympathy for her plight, however, has limitations. I take pride in a job well done. Even if it's for Valentina.

My gloating comes to an end at the sound of Viktor's gruff voice on the other side of the door. "Yo, Nicky, we have a situation."

Calliope twists beneath me. The top buttons of her blouse have popped open following our struggle, revealing the upper swells of round, supple breasts. Her chest heaves from exertion. The amount of hatred in her brown eyes is frightening. I shout over my shoulder. "I'm busy. Take care of it."

"I think you're gonna want to deal with this yourself."

"Fine." After swiping a hand over my face, I stand, pulling my captive to her feet with me. With a hand on her chest, I push her onto the bed, She falls on her back, a tide of crimson coloring her cheeks. The mattress bounces beneath her fall. "Now, you stay put and be a good girl. I'll be back in a minute." In a few quick jerks, I remove my tie and stuff it between her lips. A low growl of frustration accompanies her attempts to test the strength of the zip ties around her wrists and ankles. Stubborn girl.

In the hallway, Vik cocks an eyebrow at my rumpled shirt and the closed bedroom door. "She giving you problems, boss? Want me to take care of her?"

"No. Of course not." I pause at the nearest mirror to straighten my shirt and smooth a hand over my hair which is perfect—as always. "What's the problem?"

"The cops are on their way up." The words have barely left his mouth when the doorbell echoes through the penthouse. A frisson of anxiety tightens in my gut. Vik watches me with cool amusement. Bastard. I've hated that fucker since the first time we met. He's only here because Valentina doesn't trust me. If I step out of line, he'll be on the phone with her and Milada will be on a plane to Colombia.

By the time we reach the foyer, two uniformed policemen are standing on the slate floor in front of the double entry doors. The tallest officer steps forward, badge in hand. "Mr. Tarnovsky? I'm Officer Wilkes, and this is my partner Officer Mills."

"It's one o'clock in the morning, gentlemen, and I'm a little busy. What can I do for you?" This isn't the first time the police have visited my doorstep. Although they hold no power over me, their presence places a definite crimp in my plans for the young woman in the bedroom.

"I apologize for the late hour, sir." The officers shift apart, revealing a slender teenaged girl. Raindrops glisten on the rich, brown waves cascading over her shoulders. "This young lady says her parents are out of town and she's staying with you. Is that true?"

"Milada?" The girl lifts turbulent gray eyes to meet mine. The same eyes I see in the bathroom mirror each morning. A knife of pain twists in my chest. I clear my throat. "She's my niece." The lie hurts every time I say it.

"Well, sir, your niece and a few of her friends were picked up in a traffic stop a few blocks from here. The driver has been charged with driving under the influence of alcohol and minor consumption. There were two other minors in the car and a case of beer." The officer glares at me. Milada's gaze drops to the floor. "She says her father is Roman Menshikov. Is that true?"

The knife in my gut drives deeper. "Yes. He's my brother."

"Given that Mr. Menshikov is such a high-profile businessman and patron of the police department, we didn't want to take her to the station out of courtesy to him."

"What were you thinking?" I ask.

An unapologetic glower meets my question. "I'm so sick of school and all their rules."

I lift a hand to stop her excuses. "Never mind. We'll talk about this later." She's so like me. The realization takes my breath away. I want to be angry at her, but I can't.

"At the very least, she's guilty of minor possession, resisting arrest, and battery on a police officer." The officer keeps talking, like I care what he thinks.

"That's not true." Anger vibrates through her voice. "He put his hands on me, Uncle Nicky. What was I supposed to do? Let him touch me? And I didn't know about the beer. I don't even know those kids."

"Hush." I shoot her a warning glare. She falls silent. A scowl scrunches her forehead. The point of her chin sharpens. I know that look so well. "Thank you for your discretion in bringing her here, officers. I'll deal with this."

A crash echoes from the back of the apartment followed by the sound of breaking glass. Four heads snap in the direction of the guest bedroom. One of the policemen steps forward like he's going to investigate. "What's going on back there? Is there a problem?"

"It's probably the dog." Viktor shrugs. His calm, level head is one of the reasons Valentina values him so much. "Damn mutt gets into everything. Don't trouble yourself, boss. I'll go check on him." After adjusting his belt, he ambles toward the bedroom.

"Is there anything else, officers?" I motion for Milada to step forward. She halts at my side, eyes downcast once more. I curl an arm around her shoulders and pull her into my side.

"No, sir." With reluctance, the officer shifts his attention away from the ruckus and back to Milada. "I believe we're done here. You have a nice day."

"Thank you." When the door closes behind them, a sigh of relief bursts from my lips. I turn Milada to face me. "What the hell, young lady?"

"Oh, please." The shape of her mouth twists into an irritated frown. She breaks out of my hold and strides into the center of the living room on sky-high heels. Her footsteps leave damp smears on my white rug. "Like you care."

"I care that your father is going to be livid when he finds out what you've done. Don't take your coat off. I'm taking you home. Right now." Despite my warning, she shrugs out of her coat to reveal a short, sequined mini dress. "What the hell are you wearing?"

"Versace." She keeps walking, moving from the living room toward the kitchen. Through the wall of windows behind her, the lights of Manhattan twinkle amid wisps of fog and rain. "Do you have anything to eat? I'm starving."

Somehow, while I wasn't looking, she's grown from a gawky child into a beautiful girl with breasts. *Breasts.* I'm so old. The thickness in my throat makes my voice rough. “I’m calling Roman.” A second crash from the bedroom precedes Viktor’s muffled curses. For a second, I’d forgotten about Calliope. I scrub a hand over my face. “Fine. I need to deal with this. There are some premade meals in the fridge. Help yourself. I’ll be back in a second.”

The words have barely left my mouth when Calliope sprints into the room, eyes wild, zip ties dangling from her wrists. She skids on the slick hardwood, backpedaling to avoid crashing into me. Viktor follows. Blood drips from his nose. It takes both of us to wrestle her to the floor.

“Get off me. Get off!” Calliope’s irate shouts echo from the cathedral ceiling.

“Shut. Up.” I sprawl on top of her, pinning her to the floor with the weight of my body. She’s warm and soft beneath me. Her large breasts flatten against my chest. A brief, inappropriate flash of her legs wrapped around my waist causes my cock to stir. “Vik, get the real cuffs.”

“Let go of me, you bastard.” She thrashes, her knee almost connecting with my groin.

“What is it with you and my balls?” I shout.

Growls of fury rumble between us. Her forehead collides into mine, blurring my vision. “Let go or I’ll scream.”

“You’re already screaming, but go ahead. The walls are soundproofed. No one will hear you.” My vision sharpens. Vik snaps the handcuffs on her wrists. All of us are sweating and breathing hard. I stare into her eyes, expecting to find defeat. Instead, they're filled with defiance. "Either you cooperate, or I'll have Vik knock you out. Your choice."

"I'll cooperate." Her voice sounds small and resigned. The tension drains from her body. I ease away. Vik hauls her to her feet. With the flush of exertion on her cheeks, she's more lovely than ever. My admiration for her wild spirit grows with each passing moment. She's trapped in a hopeless situation, yet she continues to fight for her freedom. The cave man inside wants to tame her and make her mine. If only we had more time.

"What's going on?" Milada's gaze bounces from me to Calliope then to Vik. "Who's he?" In her right hand, she's holding a chicken drumstick. "Is this some kind of sick roleplay thing?"

"It's nothing. Go back to the kitchen." I take a moment to straighten my suit and run a hand over my tousled hair. "Vik, take our guest back to her room."

"I'm not a guest, you whacko." Calliope struggles against Vik's hold. She turns pleading eyes to Milada. "Help me. Please. I need help."

"I want a Porsche." Milada's stare breaks from Calliope's face. A mischievous smirk twists her lips.

"What?"

"White with white leather. Like the one you had. A convertible." One of her eyebrows lifts to taunt me.

"You're kidding." Vik drags Calliope down the hall. I stare at Milada, speechless for the first time in my life.

"You won't tell Daddy about tonight, and I won't tell him about the woman hogtied in your bedroom."

“You’re blackmailing me?” How did my life turn into such a shitshow? I pinch the bridge of my nose with thumb and forefinger to stave off a headache.

She plunks onto the sofa, crossing her long legs at the knee. “Absolutely.”

SEVEN

Calliope

In the morning, I'm escorted out of the penthouse by Nicky and Vik. Milada trails behind us. We travel down a private elevator to the service entrance at the back of the building. Vik shoves me into an Escalade with tinted windows. I stare at the passing street, watching the pedestrians on the busy Manhattan sidewalks. They're going to work, running errands, heading to their favorite coffee shops while I'm heading to my execution. It feels surreal, like watching a movie of someone else's life. However, this is *my* life—or what's left of it—and I have no intention of giving it up.

No one speaks to me except to bark directions. On the way, we drop the girl at a swanky private school. Afterward, we board a plane, have breakfast. Nicky sits a few seats away with his laptop in front of him and his phone to his ear, speaking in Russian. His relentless stare never leaves me. The sun hangs low in the sky by the time we land at a private tropical airport. A blast of heat enters the plane as the door opens. On the tarmac, I sway in the warmth of the sun. A humid breeze ruffles palm trees.

"Is anyone going to tell me where we are?" I ask no one in particular, not expecting an answer.

"Does it matter?" Nicky asks. The truth in his question brings the sting of tears to my eyes. I look away. My freedom might be gone, but I still have pride. I cling to it with my entire being.

"Can you loosen these handcuffs?" Red welts mar the flesh around my wrists. "My fingers are asleep."

"No," Nicky replies. "You lost all your privileges when you broke Vik's nose."

In that moment, the truth hits home. No one cares. To these men, I'm nothing more than a means to an end. Property. Trash to be taken out.

Viktor approaches with something black in his hands.

"Sorry," he grunts and drags a hood over my head.

In the next vehicle, I'm sandwiched in the back between Viktor and Nicky. I'm acutely aware of Nicky's presence. His cologne teases my nose, masculine and clean. The long length of his thigh presses against mine. The contact makes my insides squeeze in a combination of revulsion and desire. The car jolts and bounces along a rough road. Every bump, every rut, thrusts my body against his. I'm forced to brace my handcuffed hands on the seat in front of me to keep from toppling into his lap.

After a lengthy and uncomfortable ride, we come to a stop. Viktor drags the hood from my head. Nicky exits first and tugs me out of the car. The scent of sea spray and flowers hangs in the air. Ahead of me is a massive fortress wall topped by razor wire. Armed sentries flank an enormous gate. Nicky places his hands on my shoulders and turns me to face the opposite direction.

A sweeping path bordered by colorful blooms leads toward a white, modern, two-story mansion. Our feet crunch on the crushed gravel as we pass splashing fountains. Nicky leads the way. Viktor follows on my heels. Inside, the house has gilded ceilings, elaborate furnishings, marble tile, and erotic artwork. Beyond the open wall on the far side of the room, an ocean of azure spreads into infinity. Nicky comes to a halt in the center of the living room. There's something odd about his hesitance, like he doesn't want to continue. This small, almost nonexistent gesture scares me more than Viktor. Nicky doesn't like this place either.

"Come on." Viktor prods my back, urging me toward the rear of the house.

We pass through the open wall to the patio. An infinity pool stretches toward the water, its edges melting into the ocean. A woman rises from beneath the umbrella of her table. The edges of her sarong flap in the wind. Her hair is black, waist-length, and shiny. Enormous sunglasses hide her face.

"At last, you make it." Her voice is soft and pleasant, heavily inflected. "Come. Give me a kiss, Nikolay." The tension in his body is palpable. For a second, I almost feel sorry for him. He stalks forward to brush his lips on her cheek. She cups his ass with her free hand.

"Such a good little whore." A sadistic smile transforms her face from beautiful to hideous. "I see you've brought a guest. Please join me."

Viktor shoves me forward. We gather around the table. A middle-aged man wearing black shorts and a yellow polo shirt places tropical drinks in front of us. The woman lowers her sunglasses to study me with dark, emotionless eyes. They're like two holes into hell. "Welcome to my home, Calliope. I was worried you wouldn't make it. Viktor, remove those handcuffs, please. We are not barbarians."

His face wrinkles in a scowl. "I would advise against it. She's been difficult." I can't help smirking at his black eyes and busted lip.

"Where will she go?" The woman replaces her sunglasses and relaxes into her chair. I feel the weight of her gaze on me. "I have a hundred soldiers watching the perimeter. None of them will think twice about shooting a woman—especially this one."

Viktor unlocks the restraints. I rub my wrists, wincing at the pain as the blood rushes back into my fingertips. Once the sensation returns, I study her features. "I'm sorry. Have we met?"

"Oh, how rude of me! No, we haven't, but I've heard so much about you, I feel like we're old friends." She extends a hand covered in gold and diamonds. "I'm Valentina Sokolov. It's a pleasure to meet you."

My heart plummets to the floor. She's the wife of a Russian mobster and the leader of a Colombian drug cartel. Death and destruction accompany her name wherever it's spoken. Nicky was right. No one comes back from this place. "I wish I could say I'm pleased to be here, but…" I let my voice trail away.

"Has my whore been rude to you?" She cocks an eyebrow at Nicky. He's been noticeably silent since our arrival. "Do I need to punish you, Nikolay?"

The muscles in his throat work as he swallows. His features remain stoic, but a tempest brews in his eyes. I've never seen so much hatred in anyone's expression before. "Do whatever you think is necessary."

"Oh, that reminds mc. Let me introduce you to my new toy." As if on cue, a slender young man slices into the water and emerges poolside next to her. He drags himself onto the deck in a stunning display of tanned skin and rippling muscles. She trails her fingers down the center of his chest. "Everyone, I'd like you to meet Luis. Luis, say hello to my friends."

"Hello." At Luis's obedient greeting, my gaze flicks to Nicky. He's out of place in the heat with his dark suit and tie, especially next to Luis's tiny red banana hammock.

"Don't sulk, Nicky. Our time together has been amazing. I'm looking forward to having you join us in my bedroom tonight." Her red lips contort. "If you can get it up for me."

A muscle twitches in his cheek. Primal energy churns in the space around us. His right palm rests on the table, fingers clenching into a tight fist. When he speaks, the low growl of his voice sends a shiver up my spine. "I delivered your package. Now, release me from this insane bargain."

"All in good time." She stands, pushing her sunglasses to the top of her head as her chair scrapes over the cement. "Pablo, show our guests to their rooms, please."

"I'm not staying." Nicky rockets to his feet.

"You'll leave when I say you can." The anger in her tone turns placating, soothing, like she's bargaining with a child. "Go upstairs and change into something nice for me. Luis and I will wait for you in my room." The weight of her gaze lands on me. "Calliope, please enjoy the amenities of my home. I would suggest a nice, soothing bath and a good meal after your long journey. I'll have Pablo bring you something to wear. If you need anything more, you can call him on the house phone." She places a hand on Luis's firm ass. "Come along, Nicky."

T*hump.*

Thump-thump.

A woman's moan reverberates through the bedroom wall. The pounding has been going on forever. The rhythm matches the throbbing between my temples. I have no idea what's going on in that room, but it sounds like Valentina is having a fantastic time. Outside the open sliding doors of my bedroom, the moon hovers above a smooth sea. I cross to the veranda and draw in a deep breath, savoring the feel of air in my lungs, the caress of wind over my face, and the crash of waves on the beach. A rush of gratitude sweeps through me. I'm still alive. Every minute I can still draw breath means I have a chance to escape.

The door isn't locked, but there's nowhere to go. Armed guards patrol the house and the pool area. I sit in the rattan chair for hours, thinking about my sister, wondering if she's okay, if Cash will go after her next. Speculating is a waste of time. There's nothing I can do for her now except keep her out of this. Tonight, I just want to sit in peace. Tomorrow, I'll fight for my life, the same way I always have.

With a sigh, I settle deeper into the chair and try to enjoy the simple act of being. A knock on the door makes my heart leap. A few seconds later, the door opens, and Nicky walks in. He's carrying a bottle of rum and two glasses. "May I come in?" he asks.

"You're already in." I return my attention to the ebb and flow of the tide, not bothering to get out of my chair.

"I thought you might like some company." In a few long strides, he crosses the room and pulls up a chair next to me. He's wearing a thin cream linen shirt and matching shorts. The V-neck reveals his collarbone and a smattering of chest hair.

"I'm surprised you have the energy after all that fucking." Spite drips from my tone.

"Don't make assumptions. You know nothing." He

avoids my gaze while he fills our glasses halfway with liquor.

"And whose fault is that?" I accept the offered glass and take a deep drink. The rum heats my throat. I cough and frown. Maybe he's going to drug me again. I don't care. At this point, unconsciousness sounds like a gift.

"Sorry. Valentina keeps the good stuff locked up. This was all I could find."

"Doesn't matter."

"Not at this point." The wistfulness in his statement catches me by surprise. The scent of his cologne drifts between us as he rests his feet on the railing. I should be afraid of him, but I'm not. Nothing about his demeanor is threatening. To a casual observer, we probably look like friends having an evening drink. In another life, we could've been friends. A second glance at his muscular calves and thighs strips me of the notion. Lovers maybe. Friends? Never.

"We're a lot alike, you and I." He stares into the distance. The setting sun highlights his profile, the straight nose, his square jaw, and that delicious chin.

My snort echoes into the atmosphere. "Yeah, right."

"We're both pawns in Valentina's twisted games. I'm just as much a prisoner here as you are."

The hopelessness in his statement makes my stomach churn. What if he's playing me? I can't let his charisma and good looks overcome my common sense. Those traits are what got me into this mess. "I doubt that."

"Believe me, if I had a choice, I'd be on my way back to Manhattan right now."

"You're a powerful man. Why don't you just leave?"

His laughter rings across the reflective surface of the pool below us and drifts away on the wind. "Valentina has complete autonomy here. No one comes or goes without her express permission. And she's not done with me. Not yet." The bitterness in his voice strikes a chord in me. "I made a pact with her, and she's holding me to the letter of the bargain." He pauses to refill our glasses.

"What kind of bargain?"

"It's a long story. Let's just say she made threats against my niece—the girl in my apartment last night."

"Your niece means a lot to you?"

"More than anything." His chest rises and falls with a heavy sigh. Despite the lines of gravity around his eyes, a self-deprecating smirk twists his mouth. "If you got to know me, you'd learn that I'm not a horrible person. I have excellent hygiene. My wardrobe is impeccable. I'm a fantastic tipper. Last week, I gave up my cab to an old lady. I pay my taxes. Sometimes I give out new shoes to the homeless. And I always, *always* make sure that the woman comes first." He smooths a hand over his hair before turning those churning gray eyes on me. "If you and I were together, I'd make sure you came first, too—several times."

"Are you flirting with me?" The audacity of this man knows no bounds. "Here? Now?" I point to the deck of the veranda. "After everything you've done to me?"

"Isn't it obvious?" His shrugs. "Bringing you here was purely business." His gaze travels over my bare legs, my breasts, and stops on my mouth. "But I've wanted you since the masquerade."

"You must have some kind of super-duper libido if you're ready to go again after that marathon with Valentina."

"Like I said, you know nothing. We haven't had sex in months." His shoulders tense. "To be honest, I can't get it up around her anymore. She's too repulsive." A shudder travels through his torso. "The only thing she wants now is to humiliate me. She made me watch while Luis fucked her and pointed out all the millions of ways his technique is superior to mine." The words tumble out with a grimace, like they taste bad on his tongue. "More power to him. For his sake, I hope she tires of him quickly." He drains the glass and refills it. "I've been her whore for five long years. Now, thanks to you, I'll be released from our arrangement." He lifts his glass in a toast. "Hopefully."

"Why are you telling me this?" When he doesn't answer, I swallow past the knot in my throat. "Oh." I curl my bare toes into the jute rug. He's confiding in me because I won't be around to tell anyone.

"For what it's worth, I admire your spirit. As someone facing their final hours, you seem remarkably calm." The chair groans as he shifts to face me. "Aren't you frightened?" Without waiting for an answer, he adds, "You should be."

"I'll never give up. Not until I'm six feet under."

He stares at me for a long time. With each passing second, my pulse escalates. Such a beautiful man. Despite my hatred for him, I'm intrigued. He drops his feet to the floor, preparing to stand. "I should go."

"No. Wait." The thought of spending my last night alone brings the sting of tears to my eyes. The request bubbling past my lips shocks me. "Please stay. I could use the company. Unless that's not allowed?"

The last sliver of the sun shimmers on the horizon, preparing to sink into the calm waters. The gray of his eyes reminds me of a misty morning. He breaks his stare, shifts back in the chair, and takes another drink. "I've always been a rule breaker." For the first time since we met, a true smile lights up his face. The dimples in his cheeks deepen. "Would you like to go for a walk with me?"

EIGHT

Calliope

I should be tired, but sleep seems out of the question. Instead, I'm walking with Nicky, barefoot in the sand. The pristine beach stretches for miles in each direction. Lush jungle surrounds the edges of the compound. White cabanas dot the beach. At first glance, this could be a luxury resort. The idyllic setting is spoiled by armed sentries who watch as we make our way down to the water. Nicky wades into the surf until the foam laps at his ankles. I stand a few yards away.

"The water's warm. Join me." He beckons with an outstretched hand. The liquor bottle is tucked beneath the opposite elbow.

"No thanks. I'm fine here." I drop to the sand, crossing my legs beneath me. The nearby guard shifts his AK47 from one shoulder to the other. Nicky returns, sits beside me, and offers the rum bottle. I shake my head.

"Suit yourself." His elbows rest on his uplifted

knees. Dark, wiry hair sprinkles his muscular thighs and calves—the perfect amount. Our shoulders brush against each other. The contact lifts the tiny hairs on my skin. I shiver then rub my bicep to disperse the lingering attraction. He raises an eyebrow. "What?"

"Who are you? I mean, really."

"Nobody." The muscles of his throat convulse as he swallows.

"A nobody doesn't live in a Manhattan penthouse and rub shoulders with the Colombian cartel."

With a manicured index finger, he picks at the label on the liquor bottle. "It's the way I grew up. I never really had a choice."

"Me neither." Maybe we're more alike than I care to admit. "I did what I had to do in order to survive. Do you have any regrets in life?" The question pops out of my mouth. How strange that in the face of death my greatest regrets aren't the things that I've done, but the ones left unfinished.

"Millions. Hence the liquor."

"Give me that." I reach for the bottle, second-guessing my previous decision to remain sober. "There are a lot of things I wish I'd done. Sex on the beach. Skydiving. Horseback riding. Learning a second language. Falling in love. Finishing high school."

"Love. Yuck. An emotion I find highly overrated." He grimaces like the word tastes sour. "Jumping out of a perfectly good plane seems insane to me. And horses, in my experience, are smelly, obstinate beasts. But sex on the beach? It can be amazing. A word of warning, though. If you're not careful, you'll be digging sand out of your crevices for the better part of a week."

A rusty laugh bubbles up my throat. The sound surprises me. I haven't laughed in years. And now, in my darkest hour, I can't seem to stop. The irony of life never ceases to amaze me.

Nicky shifts back, resting his elbows in the sand. "The security wall goes around the entire compound." His tone drops to a quiet murmur, barely audible above the swish of the receding tide. The sudden shift in topic catches me off guard. I lean toward him to catch his words. "The only exits are through the front entrance or the service gate in the back. You'll never get out the front. Too many cameras and too many people. But the back gate? The sentries change three times a day at random hours. Most of the drug shipments come in on Tuesday nights. If you're going to escape, that would be the way, when they're distracted."

His tip makes my situation seem very real. "Are you saying there's a chance of escaping?"

"The odds are against you. I'm saying, if—and I do mean *if*—you were to try it, that would be the best time."

After that, we sit in silence, observing the moon drift above the water, listening to the rustle of palm leaves and the rhythmic churn of the ocean. From the corner of my eye, I watch the wind ruffle his hair. With his hair tousled and his shirt unbuttoned, he's hotter than ever. How strange that my greatest enemy has become my only ally.

"Do you think…?" My voice trails away. I clear my throat and try again. "This might seem weird, but would you kiss me?" His gaze slants to meet mine. "After the masquerade, I couldn't stop thinking about your kiss." One corner of his mouth curls upward like a comma. Then his focus dips to my mouth. A lightning bolt of desire strikes my core. "It's just—this whole deal is so surreal, and I need to feel connected to someone."

His chest rises and falls with a deep breath. He shoves a hand through his hair then wraps his fingers around my neck, digging his grip into my nape, angling my head so that my lips align with his. My heart pounds against my ribs as his face lowers to mine. Our eyes meet. The connection jolts through me. The truth smashes into me. We *are* alike. Damaged. Wounded. Obstinate.

Instead of kissing me, he brushes his lips over mine from left to right in a soft caress. The gentle sweep of velvety flesh against flesh ignites hundreds of tiny explosions beneath my skin. A quiet whimper slips out of my throat. With the tip of his tongue, he traces the Cupid's bow of my upper lip. The movement is sensual, erotic, and filled with heat. Then his tongue dips into my mouth, sliding along mine. He's slow and leisurely, like we have all the time in the world. Like this is our first kiss instead of our last. The bittersweet notion brings the prickle of tears.

When he pulls back, I'm dizzy and breathless. I open my eyes to find him staring down at me. He brushes my hair back from my face in a tender, wistful gesture. It would be so easy to pretend he's my lover. That we're starting this journey instead of ending it. He releases my neck, rises to his feet, and extends a hand. "Come on."

This is wrong on so many levels. He's the enemy. My common sense is compromised by the situation, the armed guards, Valentina's veiled threats. No one in her right mind would consider sleeping with the man who delivered her to the devil. But I've never been the type of girl to overthink things. Right now, I want to revel in the picturesque scenery and this delicious, complicated, sinful man. So, I thread my fingers through his and let him pull me toward the largest of the cabanas.

The white canvas sides flutter against the wooden posts. Inside, a rug covers the slatted deck floor. In the center, fluffy white pillows and throws cover a round wicker daybed. He grips the hem of his shirt with both hands and drags it over his head. I trail my fingertips over the ripples of his abdomen. He's taut and toned in all the right places. A small, circular scar mars the delectable cut of muscle above his hipbone. Although I can't quite make out the symbol, I know what it is. A brand. I've seen them before. On myself. I trace the edge with a fingertip.

"Her initials," he says, his tone nonchalant, like he's talking about the weather instead of abuse. I bend down to see the letters V and S joined by a circle. "She likes to inflict pain. That's how she gets into a man's head. She knows how vain I am about my looks and wanted to ruin my self-image. So that every time I look at myself in the mirror, I'll think of her."

"I'm sorry she did this to you." I place a kiss on the scar. He shudders at the touch of my lips to his skin.

"There's nothing to be sorry for. She tried to break me and failed." His warm hands slide over my bare shoulders. I'm wearing the white bikini and sarong Pablo brought to my room. Practically naked. "She'll try to break you, too."

"I don't want to talk about it. Not right now." I smooth my palms up his chest, enjoying the heat and hardness of his torso. Standing this close to him does strange things to my body. My senses are heightened by the small space, his scent, the swish of the tide.

The press of his lips to my neck sends shivers of need down my back. While his mouth trails along my collarbone, his fingers tug the strings holding my bikini top and bottoms together. The material whispers to the floor. He steps back. The length of his erection tents the front of his shorts. His attention wanders over my aching breasts, down to the triangle of hair between my legs, and back to my face. "You're lovely, Calliope."

"So are you." The words die in my throat. He yanks me to his chest. His fingers dig into the flesh at my hips, holding me against his arousal.

"When I saw you at the masquerade, I wanted to fuck you right then and there. If Roman hadn't interrupted us, I would have." Our mouths crash together. There's nothing gentle or sweet about this kiss. It's brutal. Hungry. Desperate like me.

He walks me backward toward the bed. We fall onto the mattress in a tangle of limbs. I shove his shorts down, pushing them along the length of his legs with my feet. His skin is so hot. It feels like fire against my bare belly. I dig my fingers into his hair to deepen our kiss. My worries evaporate. I throw myself into enjoying each and every sensation.

"I like your breasts." To demonstrate his approval, he nuzzles the nearest nipple, teasing it with the tip of his nose. I hiss when he sucks the tip, stretching it to a taut peak with his teeth. The sting carries the perfect balance of pleasure and pain. Pain to let me know I'm still alive, and pleasure to ease the torture.

"Thanks." His genuine appreciation makes it easy to forget that I haven't shaved my legs in days. Funny how the little things don't matter when you're facing down your mortality.

The mattress dips as he rolls to his side. His lips and tongue tease mine while his hand slides between my legs. I'm slick and needy and eager to have him inside me. He dips a finger between my folds to find my clit. With expert precision, he strokes through the sensitive flesh. Each circle—each pinch—makes me squirm. My chest heaves. I struggle to breathe as the pleasure builds into a tempest of sensation.

"Do you like that? Does it feel good?" He stares down at me, gray eyes intense. "Do you want me to continue?"

"Yes." I grip his wrist to slow down his frantic pace.

My legs jerk at the shocks of ecstasy evoked by his touch.

"Let go of me." His words are an order, not a request.

"I'm going—going—I'm going to come." It's too soon. I wanted this to last.

"Look at me, Calliope." My gaze flits up to meet his. The moonlight highlights the planes and angles of his cheekbones and jaw.

"It's too much." Every muscle in my body tenses. "I can't."

"You can, and you will." His tone is commanding, sharp. I unclench my hand from his arm. He plunges two fingers into me, deep enough to make me jerk into a sitting position. And then, I'm coming, coming, *coming*. Hard enough to blot out the future. Intense waves of bliss radiate from my core to the tips of my toes. He rides out the contractions, shaking his hand, wiggling his fingers, wringing every single drop of orgasm from my pussy.

I flop back onto the mattress. My laboring breaths echo in the stillness. He shifts on top of me, spreading my thighs with his knees, and plunges into my still quivering channel. The force drives my knees to his waist. When he's fully seated, he keeps pushing. The friction of his long cock against my walls chases away any lingering regrets. I drag my nails down his back. His hiss of pain is almost as satisfying as my previous orgasm.

"Easy with the claws, kitten." To underscore his

point, he withdraws and jabs into me again. "Or I'll have to punish you."

"If you're trying to scare me, you need to try harder. I like it rough."

"Let me put that to the test." Transferring his balance to the left, he loops his right arm through my knee, boosting my leg to my shoulder. The position leaves me open and vulnerable. He begins pounding into me. The force shoves me higher on the bed until the top of my head hits the backboard. I brace my hands against the wicker.

This is what I needed. Someone ruthless and dark to drive away my worries. I watch a dozen different expressions flit across his features: concentration, anger, pleasure, and determination. He throws his head back, riding me like his life depends upon it. And maybe it does. Maybe I'm saving him the same way he's saving me. The thought transports me to a different level of sexual awareness. The veins in his biceps swell and thicken. I sink my teeth into the tender spot where his neck meets his shoulder. He grunts from the pain. The furrow in his brow deepens. Reaching between us, he presses the pad of his thumb on my clit. It's enough to send me spiraling out of control. I gasp his name, surprised by the intensity of my climax. He stills. A shudder ripples through his body. The reaction is primal, fierce, and like catnip to me.

I close my eyes to sever the connection between us. I can't afford to feel any emotion toward this man. Despite everything, he's still the enemy. His large hand closes around my jaw, forcing my face toward his. "Open your eyes. Look at me."

Sensations collide and tumble over each other. The scratch of his hairy legs on the backs of my thighs. The brutality of his cock in my quivering pussy. Scents of sex and tropical blossoms. The crash of waves on the beach. I open my eyes, giving in to his command, to find his face inches from mine. I try to look away, frightened by what I see in those enigmatic gray irises. Fury. Triumph. Despair. A tear leaks out of the corner of my eye, rolls down my cheek. He licks it up before pressing the tenderest of kisses to my mouth.

"I'm happy to see my sexual prowess has moved you to tears." He rolls off me, but I can tell he's dealing with his own set of emotions.

We lie side by side, panting. In front of us, the vastness of the ocean spreads into infinity. Stars twinkle in a velvet sky. Once my racing heart resumes a reasonable cadence, I lift onto my elbows. Nicky trails his fingertips along the length of his sternum, face inscrutable. "We didn't use a condom. I apologize."

"It's okay. I can't have kids, if that's what you're worried about."

"Have you been tested recently?" There's a note of concern in his voice.

"Yes." I don't want to tell him that I haven't had sex in almost a year.

"So have I. And I always use a condom. At least, always before."

"Even with Valentina?"

"Especially with Valentina." The mention of her name dampens the magic of the moment. He sits up and runs his hands through his hair, smoothing the tousled ends. I expect him to make an excuse to leave, but he doesn't. Instead, he turns to me. "Would you like to go to my room? Now that I've had a taste of you, I'd like some more."

NINE

Calliope

Breakfast is served by the pool at one of thc umbrella tables. It's already hot. The humidity turns my curls into an uncontrollable frizz. Nicky and Luis are already seated. To my relief, Viktor is absent. Valentina greets me with a smile and a kiss on the cheek. "Good morning, Calliope. How did you sleep?"

"Very little." I slide into the empty chair across from Nicky. My thigh muscles tremble under the effort, pushed to their limits by hours of fucking. Valentina watches me with doe eyes. Her familiarity disturbs me on several different levels. I've known people like her. The sweet façade hides the danger of a viper.

"Did darling Nicky keep you up all night? He's a stallion, isn't he?" She drags her fingers through his hair, ruffling the brown locks like he's a pet. A pair of black aviator shades hides his eyes. He remains silent. She gives his face a playful slap. "He can go for hours with that massive cock of his." The tension at the table makes the air heavy. Her focus returns to me. "Did he do that thing with his thumb? Where he flicks your clit? I taught him that." She strokes a hand down my arm. My stomach churns. I flinch away from the unwelcome contact. A sadistic smile bows her red lips. "Maybe I'll have both of you join us in bed tonight. Wouldn't that be fun, Luis? The four of us together?"

"I'll pass." I wish I had sunglasses to hide my bloodshot eyes. Nicky looks like he just stepped off the cover of a men's fashion magazine, his face clean shaved, his white shirt starched and brilliant against his tanned skin.

"So angry. Why is that, Calliope?" With a petulant smirk, she places fresh fruit onto her plate. "You remind me of Nikolay. All brooding and stormy."

"Maybe it's just me, but being held prisoner in a foreign country always makes me cranky." Following her lead, I dish a ladle of scrambled eggs onto my plate. Across the table, Nicky's lips curve upward.

"He has a terrible temper, you know. Especially when he's forced to be submissive." Ignoring my statement, she bites into a succulent plum. "What about you, Calliope? What makes you angry?"

"Let the games begin," Nicky murmurs.

"Pollution. People who don't recycle. Runny mascara." At my answer, her laughter rings through the air.

She shakes her head and relaxes into her chair, crossing her slender legs at the knee. "You're delightful. This is going to be so much fun."

“For you, maybe.” The eggs curdle in my stomach. A chill rolls over me followed by a flash of heat. From anger. I drop my fork on the table.

She stabs at her eggs. “Oh, darling, I’m the only one who matters.”

“As much as I’d like to stay, I need to be going. I have business to take care of.” Nicky’s deep voice hits me between the legs. He pushes back his chair to stand. I press my thighs together at the unexpected pulse of desire. Last night, when we returned to his room, he’d been gentle. Bringing me to orgasm over and over again with his fingers and tongue and that enormous dick. Afterward, he’d held me in his arms, his chest to my back, spooning me until daybreak. The memory brings a flush of heat to my face.

“When I’m ready for you to leave, I’ll let you know.” Valentina’s pretty face turns ugly. “Sit down.” He doesn’t move. In a blur of motion, she snatches my head by the hair, drawing my face to hers, and presses the tip of her knife into my jugular vein. “I said sit. Now.”

“Go ahead. She means nothing to me.” His declaration stings more than the tip of the blade pricking my skin. The magic of last night ebbs away like the outgoing tide. There’s a tickling sensation along the side of my neck. I bite the inside of my cheek to keep from crying out. No matter what happens, I won’t give her the satisfaction.

“Sit down, Nicky, or I will gut her like a pig in front of your very eyes.”

Slowly, he reclaims his seat at the table.

Valentina lowers the knife. "He's a cold bastard, isn't he?" She wipes the blood—my blood—on her linen napkin then begins peeling the apple. That small gesture terrifies me more than anything I've ever experienced. She's so nonchalant about death.

"We had a bargain. I fulfilled my part. It's time to let me go," Nicky growls through clenched teeth. The armed soldier standing at the edge of the pool lifts the muzzle of his gun and inches closer to us.

Valentina's calm façade snaps. She springs to her feet, overturning her chair in the process. The table jumps as she slams both hands on the surface. "I make the rules. I say who comes and goes here. You do not tell me what to do, Nikolay." Her lips tremble with the force of her fury. "Guard!" The sentry marches to the table and lowers the muzzle of the gun to Nicky's temple.

To Nicky's credit, his expression never changes. "Go ahead. Put me out of my misery. Death would be preferable to spending one more minute in this hell hole with you."

They stare at each other for what seems like hours. No one speaks. My stomach churns. I fight against the need to heave in the bushes next to my chair. Valentina scowls. "What happened to you, Nicky? You used to be so much fun."

"You. You're what happened." Steel and fire forge together in his terse words.

The hideous reality of my future takes on a frightening twist. I'm going to die here, and it's going to be long and slow and painful.

"Ah, Viktor. There you are, sleepy head." Valentina's demeanor switches seamlessly from psychotic to delighted. "Come join us."

The hulking Russian skirts the edge of the pool. If he's surprised by the state of affairs, he doesn't show it. He slides into the empty chair next to me and unfolds a napkin onto his lap. "Good morning."

"Take Calliope to the house, would you?" Valentina addresses the guard, her demeanor pleasant. The man lowers the gun from Nicky's head and uses the barrel to gesture for me to get up. "I have a full day planned for you. Massage, facial, manicure, pedicure. The whole spa treatment. My treat." Pushing my chair back from the table, I stand. This bitch is certified crazy. Nicky avoids my gaze. She gestures with the knife. "Oh, and Pablo, move Calliope into Nicky's room."

I'm taken to a conservatory filled with blooming flowers, fruit-bearing trees, and caged birds. A waterfall splashes onto bright blue tile in the far corner. An aesthetician gestures for me to lie on a massage table. Her assistant hands me a glass of champagne. I have no idea what to think. The scene is decadent and relaxing, but I know better than to trust my eyes. Throughout the procedures, a sentry guards the exit. I have no choice but to comply.

I recognize how silly it sounds to be tortured by way of pampering. At the end of the day, my body is relaxed, hairless, and glowing, but my mind reels. Valentina is plotting something. On the walk back to the bedroom, I scan the house, memorizing the exits, searching for cameras and a way to freedom.

The guard locks me in Nicky's bedroom. The space is simple but comfortable with an enormous king-sized bed, two overstuffed chairs, and a veranda. I search through the dresser drawers for a weapon but only find Nicky's clothing and a variety of bikinis for me. The closet holds even less: a few pairs of shoes for him, sandals for me, and wood hangers. I remove one from the bar and test the weight of it in my hand. A few minutes later, the door opens. Whirling to face the intruder, I brandish the hanger like a weapon.

"Easy." Nicky closes the door behind him. The place is in shambles. Our clothes litter the floor. Drawers are open. The bed covers and mattress are askew. "Calliope, calm down." He extends a hand, as if to soothe a skittish horse.

"Don't tell me to calm down." I continue holding the hanger between us. "That bitch is looney tunes."

"Get hold of yourself." Nicky grabs me by the biceps and gives me a shake. I drop the hanger. It lands on the tile floor with a clatter. "You're not going to take out an entire army with a piece of wire."

"I know." My body trembles. I grip my head, unable to stop the panic spreading through my chest. "I know. I *know*."

He releases my arms and sinks into the bed. Lines of worry bracket his mouth. "Freaking out isn't going to help."

“Is this room bugged?” I run my hands over the lampshade and picture frame then pace in front of the window. The tightness in my chest increases until my ribs creak. No, no, no. It’s been so long since I’ve had a panic attack.

“Maybe. Probably.” He runs his hands through his hair, tousling the glossy brown locks. “This is exactly what she wants. Your fear. Don’t give her the satisfaction.”

“What is she planning?” I wrap my arms around my waist, seeking comfort that never arrives. “I spent the day being groomed like a prized poodle. Why are we in this room together?”

“I can only guess, but I suppose she plans to pit us against each other.” His heavy sigh says more than words. “It’s a common form of mental torture. She forces us to form a bond then tears the relationship apart.”

“We’re fucked, aren't we?” It's not really a question. And he knows it. I resume pacing. This is beyond all comprehension. “I don't even know what I'm doing here.”

“Are you sure? You've done something to pique her interest. Think hard. Maybe you stole something from her.”

“I'd remember someone like her.” A sliver of uncertainty takes seed in my gut. There have been so many marks over the years. Cash orchestrated the projects, choosing our targets, but never disclosing his motives. I sink down on the bed next to Nicky. "I don't know. Maybe."

A sudden, unwelcome thought infiltrates my anxiety. "Last night, did you show up on your own or did she send you to find me?" His lips press into a tight line, providing the answer. Anger threatens the shreds of my self-control. "Did she tell you to fuck me, too?"

"She sent me into your room, but only to check up on you. Everything else—the walk, the beach, sex—it was me." He rests a hand on my knee. I brush it away. "This is exactly what she wants. You and I pitted against each other. Don't play into her plans."

The past few days have been too much. My head whirls from information overload. I wish I could click my heels together and go home, back to my cramped apartment, the bar, and my anonymity. My life was a disaster, but it was mine. And Nicky is just as much a part of the game as Valentina. "I can't be around you right now."

With the door locked, there's nowhere to go, so I head to the bathroom and close the door behind me. I sit on the closed toilet and focus on my breathing. A few minutes later, I hear the bedroom door open and close. When I emerge from the bathroom, a white sundress has been laid out on the bed with matching white lace panties. And sandals with thin gold straps. Nicky is nowhere to be found. His absence is as concerning as it is a relief. I don't know what to think or who to believe.

There's a knock on the door. Pablo enters. "Mrs.

Sokolov requests that you get dressed and join her in the living room." After a brief bow, he departs.

I stare at the clothes, warring between rebellion and complicity. If I refuse, she might retaliate. If I comply, I may be attending my own death. The debate is brief. I have no choice. With a heavy heart, I change clothes. The dress is a little too short but flattering. One of the guards delivers me to the living room. Luis is seated on the sofa nibbling from a bowl of macadamia nuts. Nicky stands near the bar, a glass of liquor in his hand and a faraway stare in his eyes. Viktor watches from a shadowy corner. Valentina approaches, her hands lifted in greeting.

"Welcome, welcome." Her long dark hair is swept into a complicated updo. The slit in her slinky red dress reveals a stretch of toned thigh. "I'm so glad you decided to join us. Aren't you, Nicky?"

"Thrilled." Unrest simmers in his posture.

"I hope your rested and ready for our games tonight, Calliope. After all, you're the star of the show." She claps her hands together. I flinch at the unexpected sound. "Nicky, you will escort Calliope? Come, Luis."

Nicky says nothing but offers his elbow. I hesitate before resting my hand in the crook of his arm. His gray eyes churn like a stormy sea. The turbulence in his gaze makes my stomach twist.

On the walk to the guest house, I'm grateful for Nicky's arm. My knees feel like gelatin. Tiki torches light the pathway. Birds and unfamiliar creatures call out to each other in the surrounding jungle, reminding me of the dangers in the dark. Valentina and Luis follow close behind. And farther back, Viktor follows with a trio of sentries.

Inside the guesthouse, my heart does a triple flip. There are no furnishings. Just a series of folding chairs arranged like theater seats and two wooden chairs in the center of the room. Various hooks and rings are mounted to the walls and ceiling. On the far wall is a work bench bearing an assortment of tools.

This is not good. I want to run, but Nicky places his opposite hand over mine, holding me in place. "Steady," he whispers in my ear.

"Calliope, you sit here." She pats one of the chairs. "Nicky, here." Valentina proceeds straight to the workbench and surveys the implements. The hairs on the back of my neck stiffen. The glow of Nicky's tan has been replaced with a sickly pallor, as if he knows what happens next.

More men enter the room. Some are dressed in suits and ties. Others wear camouflage uniforms. All of them carry visible weapons. The man in the corner, however, is the one who concerns me most. A white apron is tied around his neck and waist. He's tall, thin, with a big nose and pockmarked complexion. He trails claw-like fingers over the implements until he finds one to his liking.

Victor comes forward and straps my arms to the chair. The men file into their seats, murmuring, watching me with vile smirks.

"Take off your shirt, Nicky," Valentina commands.

When he doesn't comply, she rips it open. The buttons ping along the floor. She leans on the work-bench and withdraws a cigarette from her silver case, flicks a lighter to the tip. The thin man selects a blow-torch and a long iron stick with a small circle on the end. A brand. The air in the room, it's too thin. My vision blurs. I've never been so terrified in my entire life. She takes a few puffs on the cigarette then walks over to Nicky. Her fingers trail over his bare chest, but her eyes are on me. "Are you ready to play, Calliope?"

"What's wrong with you?" I ask, twisting desperately against the leather restraints. "You're sick."

"Hush." With a hand on Nicky's chest, she shoves him into the chair facing me. Victor tightens the straps around his wrists. I can't look at him. If I do, I think I'll cry. Valentina exhales, plumes of smoke curling around her head. "Have you figured out why you're here yet?"

"I have no idea. I think you're mistaking me for someone else." The pitch of my voice is too high, strained and thin.

"No. No mistake." The heels of her sandals click on the cement as she circles me. "I want you to think really hard." She pats my face. "Victor, help her out. "

The blow comes out of nowhere. My head snaps back. The metallic taste of blood fills my mouth.

"Valentina, you don't have to do this," Nicky interrupts. "She'll tell you whatever you need to know. Violence isn't necessary."

"If you speak again without my permission, I'll silence your smart mouth. Permanently." The venom in her tone escalates my panic. She gestures with the cigarette. “I promised these men a night of entertainment, and I always keep my promises.”

“Not always,” Nicky says, taunting her. “Only when it’s to your advantage.”

“Why can’t you follow the rules, Nicky? It’s so simple. You come when you’re called. You speak when you’re spoken to. Always a rebel.” She shakes her head and draws another puff of her cigarette. “Here’s how this is going to go. Every time one of you breaks my rules, I’m going to punish the other one. What do you think, Viktor?”

The henchman nods and cracks his knuckles. “Sounds fair to me.”

The thin man fires up the blowtorch, stalking toward me without expression. I want to run. Even if I got free, there’s nowhere for me to go. My voice shakes when I speak. “I’ll tell you whatever you want to know. But I honestly don’t know what you’re talking about.”

Valentina takes a long draw on the cigarette, her flat black eyes contemplating me. Then she lowers the cigarette to Nicky’s chest. He doesn’t flinch or cry out, but a bead of sweat appears on his forehead as she presses the glowing red tip to his flesh.

“No. Stop.” I’ve never been one to beg, but I can’t bear to see someone else tortured on my account. “Please.”

Valentina nods, smiling at my answer. "What do you think, Victor?"

Victor nods his assent. "Sounds good to me, boss."

The metal legs of a chair scrape over the floor as she drags it closer to me. She takes a seat, crosses her legs at the knee, and leans forward from the seat, blocking my view of Nicky.

"Okay." Her gaze bores into me. "Calliope, you will go first." The tip of her tongue sweeps over her lower lip. "Now tell me. How old were you when your stepfather first touched you?"

TEN

Calliope

A throbbing pain in my head awakens me from a deep and dreamless sleep. I groan and throw a forearm over my eyes. For a minute, I think I'm back in my shitty apartment. Then I remember Nicky, the tropical compound, and Valentina's psychotic smile. I spring to a sitting position, scanning the space. I'm in a different room. It's dark. No windows. No furniture. Just a bucket on a hard, concrete floor. I know the door is locked, but I check it anyway.

This room is small, barely bigger than a closet. My chest heaves as I fight for air. *Breathe, Calliope, breathe.* In through the nose. Out through the mouth. The tight space reminds me of my childhood. Of the many days and nights spent locked in the closet as punishment by a junkie mother who couldn't be bothered with a rebellious kid.

Slowly, the terror of the past few hours unfolds in my hazy brain. My body aches from Viktor's brutal punches. I run my tongue around the perimeter of my mouth, grateful to find all my teeth in place. Aside from one fist to the mouth, he'd kept his blows confined to my body. Nicky hadn't been so lucky. She seemed to take pleasure from inflicting pain on his proud body.

During the worst of it, I'd taken strength from his unwavering gaze. He'd been an anchor in the midst of all the chaos. "Look at me, Jones," he'd whispered when the thin man came at me with the brand. If I had doubted his part in this fiasco before, I know the truth now. He's as much a victim as I am. How has he endured this crazy torture for five years? I can't blame him for using me to gain his freedom.

I curl up in the corner, too exhausted and weak to sit. The only sound is the beating of my heart. A tear oozes down my swollen cheek. I'm so fucked. I want to cry, but I know that once I start, I might lose control completely.

When sunshine illuminates the cracks in the door, Viktor arrives. Daylight streams into the room, blinding me. He places a bottle of water on the floor between us. Is it my imagination or has he gotten bigger overnight? I struggle to my feet and shrink to the farthest corner. "Valentina is having breakfast on the patio and wants you to join her. Put this on." He tosses a blue flowered sundress at me. "Hurry up."

"Do you mind?" I ask, hoping for a tiny bit of modesty.

"Just do it." He stands in the open doorway, arms crossed over his chest, and watches while I wash my hands and face with the water. His gaze roams over me with inappropriate zeal. Afraid to turn my back on him, I strip off the blood-spattered white dress and pull the new one over my head. We walk in silence down the winding pathway from the guesthouse to the pool. My body aches in ways I never guessed possible. The sweet scent of jasmine and magnolias turns my stomach.

At the table, Valentina removes her sunglasses and wraps a motherly arm around my shoulders. Her touch sends a shiver down my spine. "Oh, look at you. Poor baby. Does it hurt?" With the tip of a finger, she gingerly touches my swollen eye.

"What do you think?" I brush her hand away, not caring that the gesture might bring about more punishment.

"Pablo, bring some ice for this sweet girl." She pulls out a chair for me. I sit down, refusing to wince at the soreness in my muscles. Nicky arrives a few minutes later. He's dressed in loose drawstring pants and a linen pullover shirt. When he removes his sunglasses, purple and green circles rim his eyes. If he's in pain, he doesn't show it. As he sits, his gaze flicks to mine. The amount of rage in his steely gaze knocks me to the back of my seat. He hates Valentina as much or more than I do.

"Oh, don't look at me that way, Nikolay." Valentina's tone turns petulant. "You'll hurt my feelings."

"Fuck. You." The deep growl of his voice is an ominous warning.

Her shoulders rise and fall with a deep sigh. "I'm growing tired of your attitude."

"Then let me go. You got what you wanted." When she doesn't answer, he leans forward. "I have businesses to run. People will be looking for me. *Roman* will be looking for me. You don't want the war king to come here, do you?"

"That Russian has-been doesn't scare me." With a wave of her hand, she returns her attention to me. "I'm invincible."

I stare at the plate of scrambled eggs and fresh fruit on my plate. My guts ache like they did when I was in a car wreck. Even if I could eat, my stomach wouldn't accept it. I push the plate away.

"Not hungry? You need to keep up your strength. We're just getting started." At the sight of her frown, my entire body begins to tremble. I remember her punishments all too well. She shrugs. "Suit yourself. Nicky, why don't you take her up to your room and let her rest? I'm sure a nap and a long soak in the tub will do wonders for your aches, Calliope. And when you've rested, we'll continue our work from last night."

The words strike terror in my soul. Nicky stands, helps me from my chair, and rushes me into the house. He's silent until the bedroom door closes behind us.

"Are you okay?" I smooth my fingertips over his swollen lips and bruised face.

"I've been worse." The apathy slides from his expression. He draws me into his embrace, wrapping one arm loosely around my waist. The other presses my head to his chest. His touch is tender. The gentleness brings the sting of tears to my eyes. He smooths my hair, murmuring the same words over and over. "I'm sorry. So sorry."

"No. I'm sorry." The longer he holds me, the more violently my body shakes. I cling to him, taking strength from his embrace. Even though he's my enemy, I need to believe there's still kindness in the world. Because without that small glimmer of hope, I've got nothing left to keep me from falling apart. "But I had to lie. If she finds out about my sister—"

"It's okay. I understand." His breath puffs against my hair. "You need to protect her. No one will fault you for that."

Pablo brings up bath salts, a first aid kit, and more ice. The concern for our welfare is confusing. Apparently, Valentina wants healthy victims. I want to refuse, but Nicky insists. "Those cuts need tending. You don't want to get an infection. The jungle harbors all kinds of nasty germs."

In mute fascination, I let him ease me into the bathroom. He washes my face with a warm cloth, eyes narrowed in concentration. I hiss at the sting when he applies antibiotic ointment to the split in my lip and the tiny cuts left by Viktor's ring. The amount of gentleness in his touch is both comforting and arousing. On occasion, our eyes meet. The gray of his irises is liquid, mesmerizing, and soft like flannel. How would it feel to look in those eyes without the shadow of Valentina hanging over us?

ELEVEN

Nicky

The sight of Calliope's battered body is more than I can bear. Valentina has always been cruel, but it's never affected me like this. For hours, she made Calliope talk about the way her stepfather abused her, the prostitution and pornography. Throughout the entire inquisition, Calliope never broke down. Not once. She held her head high, cursing at Viktor, spitting on Valentina's designer shoes. Every time she hesitated or refused to answer, Valentina took it out on me. I was the weak one. I hate myself for doing nothing while Viktor satisfied his hatred of women with his fists.

Calliope sits on the closed toilet lid while I fill the tub with the essential oils and salts provided by Pablo. At her request, I help her undress. The burn mark from Valentina's brand glows in the same place as mine above Calliope's left hip. The water splashes as she submerges up to her chin in the soothing bath. Her eyes close, long lashes fanning out in half-moons on her cheeks.

"I'll give you some privacy." I turn, intending to let her rest and take some personal time to sort out my emotions. I never expected to feel so much empathy for a stranger.

Her hand catches my wrist. She sits up. Opens her eyes. "Thank you."

"For what? Getting you into this mess? For drugging you, kidnapping you, giving you over to an evil drug lord/human trafficker who wants both of us dead?" The depths of my self-loathing sink to an all-time low. "I sat there and watched while Viktor did this to you. I'm as bad as she is."

"She held a knife to your throat." The same knife she used to peel apples at the breakfast table. "You had no choice." The cut on my neck from the tip of the blade still stings. Calliope shakes her head, invoking ripples in the water. "She would've killed you."

The truth doesn't minimize my guilt. This shit with Valentina should have ended long ago. At first, it was honor that kept me from taking action. I'd given her my word in exchange for a favor. Back then, she was only into whips and candle wax, things I'd often indulged in at my sex club. I was a fool to think I could extract myself from her bargain without consequences. Excuses won't make this situation better, but I feel like I owe Calliope an explanation. The words knot on my tongue.

"Stop blaming yourself." Calliope speaks without opening her eyes.

"I can't help it. None of this would have happened if it wasn't for me." The guilt eats at my soul. Calliope was so brave, and I did nothing. I said *nothing*. Blood pumps faster and faster through my veins until I feel like my heart will explode. "Five years ago, when I negotiated this deal, I had no idea what I set into motion. If I had, I would have found another way."

At the time, there had been no other options. I had to stop Don McElroy before he killed the people who mattered most to me.

"Wallowing in regret isn't going to solve anything." Beneath the bubbles, the curves of her breasts are faintly visible. I try not to stare. She's been violated enough. "We need a plan."

"Believe me when I say escape is impossible. I've tried. Numerous times." And each time, the punishment of being caught was unbearable. "Her power extends way beyond this compound. The people in the villages work for her. She feeds and clothes them. Pays for their schools and hospitals. Even if you managed to get past the guards and the razor wire, someone will find you and bring you right back." I perch on the edge of the tub and run a hand over my jaw. The stubble of whiskers abrades my palm. I haven't shaved since I arrived, something uncharacteristic for me. "The only option is to wait it out. Her attention span is limited at best. After a few days, she'll lose interest. She'll let me go eventually. When I'm free, I'll do what I can to get you out of here."

"Why, in hell, would you make a bargain like this?"

"Do you remember Don McElroy?"

"The former Vice President?" She sits up a little. "The one who was involved in all that dirty stuff?"

"Yes. That one." I nod. The shenanigans of the former war hero had been plastered all over the media for months. "He threatened to kill Rourke, my sister-in-law, and her best friend Everly. I had to find him before he could carry out the plan. He took refuge here, with Valentina. I tried to bribe her to turn him over to me, but being wealthy, she wasn't interested in money. She'd been coming on to me for years, asking me to join her on vacations. I'd always refused. When she proposed a sexual relationship, I agreed. I've slept with many, many women. One more didn't seem out of the question. In fact, it seemed like an easy fix to a huge problem." At the time, the request had been a mere inconvenience. In hindsight, I should've known better. "The last time I tried to end our bargain, she threatened to kidnap Milada and bring her here." And I just couldn't have that.

With her big toe, she turns the faucet handle, adding more hot water to the steaming bath. She winces at the movement. My admiration for her grows. I've seen men twice her size cry over injuries half as serious.

"Let me get you some ibuprofen." I begin rummaging through the first aid kit.

"No, I'm fine, or at least, I will be after I kill that bitch."

At her surprising declaration, a burst of laughter

rumbles out of my chest. Her swollen mouth bows in a smile. "You impress me, Miss Jones."

"Wait until you see me in action. I'm amazing." With those final words, she lets out a sigh and tilts her head back to rest on the bath pillow.

"I can hardly wait." I head to the bedroom veranda and stare out the window at the ocean. I used to love the beach, but now the sight of sand and surf turns my stomach. With a groan, I let my head fall into my hands. There has to be a way out of this for both of us.

A short time later, Pablo arrives with lunch. His eyes avoid mine as he sets the tray on the small table next to my chair. "Mrs. Sokolov would like you to know that she's been called away on business for a few days. She asks that you enjoy the amenities of the compound in her absence."

"Thank you." I lift the lid of the largest silver chafing dish to scrutinize the contents. "Is this okay to eat?"

"Yes, sir. The food is fine, but I would avoid the iced tea."

"Great. I appreciate it." Over the years, I've cultivated a relationship with Pablo. I help him with his English and pad his income while he looks after me during my visits to this tropical hell.

"Is no problem." His gaze flits to the bathroom where Calliope can be heard moving around. "She okay?"

"What do you think?"

"Not for me to pass judgment," he replies, like he's

reading from a script. After a short bow, he backs toward the door. "If you need anything, please let me know."

Calliope returns from the bathroom, running a towel through her curly black hair. The belt of a fluffy bathrobe cinches tight around her narrow waist. "Is that lunch? I'm starving."

"Yes. Help yourself." While I'm speaking, I pour the contents of the glass pitcher into the bathroom sink.

"Why did you do that?"

"Valentina sometimes likes to put a little something extra in her food and drinks. It's always wise to be cautious. Let her drink and eat first. If you have the opportunity, you can ask Pablo."

"Why would he tell you something like that? Isn't he afraid of what will happen if she finds out?" Her brown eyes lock onto mine. For a second, I lose myself in the warmth of their depths.

"He's just as much a hostage as we are. She forced him into employment for repayment of a debt."

She sits in the opposite chair and bites into a triangle of chicken salad on toast. The damp strands of her hair float around her face. We eat in silence. Unlike before, this lack of conversation seems natural. It's a novelty to me. My previous interactions with women have been limited to flirting and sex. Although I've only known her a short time, a bond is growing between us.

"You don't like the crusts?" I point to the remnants of bread on her plate.

"No." Her pert nose crinkles. "It's disgusting."

"Is there any particular reason?" My attempt at lightheartedness receives a raised eyebrow.

"Not really." She tucks a foot beneath her and holds the sandwich with both hands, nibbling on it like a mouse. The gesture is both cute and endearing. "My gran used to cut them off for me. I guess it just reminds me of her."

"And she was good to you?" The more I know her, the more curious I am about the events that made her into such a strong woman.

"Yes. Most of the time." Our fingertips touch as we reach for the same sandwich at the same time. The electric jolt up my arm makes me flinch. She bites her teeth into the fullness of her lower lip and chooses a different one. "My mother and I lived with her until she kicked us out. Not that I blame her. Mom was a full-blow heroin addict by then."

"That must have been difficult for you."

Her shoulder lifts in a nonchalant shrug. "It is what it is. It happened, and I dealt with it. There really wasn't any other choice."

"I can relate." Although my circumstances were much different, I never felt loved or wanted, and I was forced into a life of someone else's choosing. "What about your sister? Where is she?"

"I don't know." The glimmer of tears shines in her eyes.

Beneath us, the gardening crew moves into the pool yard to perform maintenance. We watch them scurry about in their gray uniforms. The buzz of lawn equipment breaks the quiet. Pablo returns to remove the tray and dishes. Afterward, she withdraws a small tube of burn cream from her robe pocket. "I almost forgot. I found this in the first aid kit. I put it on my—the burn. You should put some on yours." She looks away, like it's too difficult to meet my eyes.

"It's not necessary. I'm fine." I shift, remembering Valentina's devious smile as she pressed the glowing tip of her cigarette to my bare skin over and over again. The odor of burning flesh. *My* flesh. Her laughter on the few occasions that my control slipped and I showed the pain.

"You just gave me a lecture about the dangers of infection in this type of environment. Open your shirt." With one hand on her hip and both eyebrows raised, she stands in front of me.

"Fine." I drag my shirt over my head and toss it on the bed. She squeezes a bit of ointment onto the tip of her finger, dabbing it gently on the worst burn. I try not to jerk at her gentle touch. To distract myself from the sting, I watch the way her brows furrow as she concentrates. When she bends to attend the wounds around my navel, her hair tickles my chest. Without thinking, I lower my head to smell the thick, shiny locks. She smells delicious—a combination of coconut, honey, and citrus. Startled, she glances up. The movement brings her face close to mine. My lips tingle with the urge to kiss her.

I shouldn't. I know better. Forming an attachment with this woman will only make us more vulnerable to

Valentina's mind games. On the other hand, the urge to live every moment to the fullest has always been a temptation I can't deny. The decision is made for me. She lifts on her toes and presses her mouth to mine. I hiss at the initial ache.

"Oh. I'm sorry." She tries to pull away.

"No. I like it." I slide a hand down to grip her round bottom. It takes great effort to keep my kiss gentle.

Her fingers wrap around my biceps for balance. "I don't want to hurt you any more than I already have."

I pull back and let my hands drop to my sides. Even though I want more of her, both of us are emotionally raw. "You should rest. Why don't you sleep for a while?"

"No." Her gaze flits to the floor then out the window. Fear flickers across her face.

"She's out of town on business for a few days. You can relax."

The tension visibly eases from her body. "Well, maybe. Only if you'll stay with me. In case—in case I wake up and don't know where I am."

"Are you sure?" The bed beckons behind us, comfy and soft. Exhaustion seeps into my muscles.

A rare smile brightens her face. She drops the robe to the floor. Beneath it, she's wearing one of my shirts. The sight of her in my clothes gives me a primal pang of ownership. She's not mine, but I'd claim her in a heart-beat. Her legs are long and shapely, her ass round and sweet. The mattress dips as she slides between the covers then pats the bed beside her. "Come on. Don't be scared."

"All right. Let's do this." I toe off my shoes before joining her.

"I'm afraid I'll have nightmares if I close my eyes. Last night brought back bad memories." She turns on her side away from me. Her voice is so soft that I have to lean closer to catch her words. "I went to live with my stepfather when I was fourteen because Mom was in rehab. He—he used to lock me in the closet for punishment. And sometimes, when I talked back, he'd burn me with his cigarette. Last night—being in that tiny room, watching Valentina hurt you—it made all those terrible memories come rushing back."

The vision of a young, frightened, curly-haired girl alone in the darkness tugs at my cold and withered heartstrings. Because I don't know what else to say, I ease my chest against her back, wrap an arm around her waist, and pull her to me. A sigh of contentment whispers from her lips. She's warm and soft and fits perfectly into the curve of my body. "Don't worry. I'll be right here to chase the nightmares away."

The next time I wake, the sun is low on the horizon. Calliope is stretched out next to me, one arm thrown over her head, lips slightly parted. The bruises on her face have progressed to deep shades of purple, green, and yellow. I smooth the hair from her face, careful not to wake her. A wave of tenderness rolls through me. The foreign feeling spreads warmth through my chest.

Calliope sighs and nestles deeper into my embrace.

The shirt rides up her back, putting her bare bottom against my groin. My cock, which has always had a mind of its own, stiffens. Holy hell. What is she doing? Her hips move in a slow circle. My breath hitches. "Calliope."

"Hush." Her voice is rough from sleep. "Just go with it."

One of her hands finds my thigh. I slide a hand beneath her shirt—*my* shirt—to find her breast. Her nipple puckers at the brush of my thumb. A growl rumbles up my throat. Everything about her draws me in: her scent, her softness, the way her body fits mine. She pushes against me. My cock slides between her folds. She's slick and wet, ready for me. I glide into her, one inch at a time.

"Your pussy is so tight." I whisper the words in her ear, savoring her tiny grunt of satisfaction when I'm fully buried inside her. I keep my movements slow and gentle. After Valentina's abuse, this needs to be good for her. We rock together. I withdraw and push back in, taking my time. Each thrust culminates in sweet agony. I could go on forever like this. My testicles tighten as my orgasm builds. Valentina and Viktor fade into nonexistence. There is only me, Calliope, and the gentle smack of my pelvis against her bottom.

"I'm going to come." Her voice breaks on the last word.

"Not yet." I pinch her nipple, twisting it, reveling in the hiss of her breath. Her walls clench in response. The way she reacts to my touch serves as the most potent aphrodisiac I've ever known. Although I take pride in my lovemaking techniques, my motives have always been selfish. The more a woman enjoys herself, the better the sex is for me. But this—this is different. This is for both of us.

"Too late." The sharp edges of her fingernails dig into my leg. Her pussy flutters around me, clutching and clenching. My climax arrives in a rush of fire through my veins when she cries out my name.

TWELVE

Calliope

For the next hour, Nicky holds me in his arms. The strength of his embrace makes it easy to pretend that we're a normal couple and not Valentina's captives. We chat about mundane things like music and art. He's easy to talk to and listens with interest. No man has ever cared about my opinions, not since Cash. Thinking about my ex-boyfriend and former employer stirs up emotions I don't care to deal with right now. Hours later, our conversation drifts into silence broken only by his measured breathing, and we sleep.

Pablo arrives with a breakfast tray and announces that we're free to roam the property today. Knowing Valentina will be absent eases a bit of the tension in my gut. I need time to formulate a plan and prepare myself for her return. The last few hours have cemented my resolve. She *will not* break me. Buoyed with hope, I crawl out of Nicky's arms and into the shower.

"Mind if I join you?" He steps into the steamy spray of water without waiting for my answer.

"Suit yourself," I reply, moving aside to give him room beneath the dual waterfall showerheads. As much as I like him, I can't allow myself to feel anything but fondness. However, sometime during the past twenty-four hours, he's moved from enemy to friend.

In the bright light of day, I feel shy in front of him about my tummy bulge, the heaviness of my breasts. He seems oblivious to my self-consciousness. Through lowered lashes, I watch as he drizzles soap on a loofah and begins scrubbing. This whole situation is beyond surreal. We're virtual strangers—enemies—held captive in a tropical paradise. Yet, I can't help admiring the ripple of water over his lean body. His casual demeanor suggests he's done this with more than one woman. A sliver of jealousy arises at the idea. Which is ridiculous. If I'm going to survive this ordeal, I can't fall for him. So, I turn my back to finish washing and get dressed.

"Where are you going?" he asks. Damp strands of hair cling to his temples as he pushes his arms into his shirt and adjusts the collar. The contrast between the buttoned-up man at the bar and this casual, tousle-haired guy makes me do a doubletake.

"I need to know what I'm working with." Now that the shock of being kidnapped has faded, my old persona —the one I had fought so hard to extinguish—comes back to life with a vengeance. "I want to see the security system, check out the perimeter wall, and look for vulnerabilities." His eyebrow lifts. I ignore his questioning gaze. "If working with Cash taught me anything, it's that every fortress has a weak spot."

"Not this one."

"People said that about Bellingham Manor, but I was able to find a way in there." Although I'd been forced to do that job, the success of our mission still gave me pride.

"That was a fluke. You caught us at a bad time. I can assure you that will never happen again."

"Well, you can't expect me to just sit in this room and wait for her to come back. Maybe you're content to do nothing, but I'm not." I tie a bright sarong around my hips to cover my bikini bottoms. "Does she have a computer or phones? There has to be something we can use."

In two strides, he crosses the room and grabs me by the biceps. He gives me a brutal shake. "Listen to me. I've walked every inch of this place. There is no escaping. All you're going to do is piss her off and make it worse."

"If I listened every time someone told me it wasn't possible, I would never have been successful at anything."

His hands slide from my arms, palms lingering over my bare skin. Gooseflesh pebbles along my forearms. Being in close proximity has awakened some kind of magnetic force between us. I can't help missing his touch the moment it's gone.

"Stubborn." He shakes his head, sending droplets of

water onto his shirt. Free of gel, the ends of his hair curl up in rebellious disarray.

"You bet your sweet ass."

A mischievous smile brightens the darkness on his face. "You think my ass is sweet?"

Except for our bedroom, all of the doors in the enormous house are locked. Downstairs, we have access to the common areas. All the drawers and cabinets are locked or empty. Cameras surveil every square inch of floor space. Some are visible in the ceilings. Others have been strategically planted in fake books, sculptures, and plants. It takes several hours to comb the house. Four more hours to scour the pool area, the garden, and lawns.

"She's been very thorough." I can't hide the disappointment in my voice.

"I don't want to say I told you so, but—" Nicky has followed me patiently throughout my quest, keeping his thoughts to himself until we stop in front of the courtyard fountain. Two bare-breasted mermaids hold a pineapple on uplifted arms. Water splashes over their naked torsos. He sits on the edge of the tiled basin, hands in the pockets of his shorts, and studies me. "She's probably watching us right now." In response, I turn to the nearest camera and lift my middle finger. He chuckles. "Easy now, spitfire."

"Don't do that." My temper, which has been hiding

beneath my bruises, rallies at his laughter. "Don't patronize me. Maybe you're okay with our situation, but I'm not."

"You still don't understand." With an angry growl, he jumps to his feet.

"Then explain it to me." I open my mouth to say more, but he interrupts by stalking toward me.

"This game only ends one way. Her way." The fury in his voice causes my mouth to snap shut. "Do not underestimate the lengths she will go to. You have no idea."

"Tell me." Now I'm angry, too. I stand, moving closer until the tips of my sandals meet the toes of his deck shoes, and stare into his gray eyes. "Because I'm dying to understand."

He edges closer. The tip of his nose hovers millimeters from mine. "The first night I came here as part of the bargain, there was someone else here. A woman. Her name was Valerie. She'd been here for almost a year. I never saw her again after that night. Pablo said they took her out to sea and she never came back." His gaze turns cloudy and distant as he gazes at the bright blue ocean. "I think about her sometimes. Who she was. Where she came from. And I wonder if anyone misses her."

Acid churns in my stomach. *A year?* "How could anyone survive this hell for so long?" Then I remember the length of his servitude to the Colombian cartel queen.

"She had no choice. Just like you have no choice."

His broad chest rises and falls with a deep breath. He backs away, running both hands through his hair.

"Oh." The strength ebbs from my knees. A new respect begins to build for him. I can't imagine leaving this place then returning of my own accord. Only a man of great character and internal fortitude could do such a thing. All because he loves his family more than he values his life. I can forgive him for bringing me here. In his shoes, I would do the exact same thing.

THIRTEEN

Calliope

The next day, I continue searching. Nicky accompanies me, probably out of boredom. I don't mind. I like having him around. Not only is he easy on the eyes, but his dry sense of humor and intelligence intrigue me. The occasional brush of his shoulder against mine as we walk the garden pathways is enough to make my core tingle in delight. Together, we watch the habits of the sentries, try to engage the staff in conversation, and scour the property for potential weak spots. I don't want to give up hope for escape, but I haven't found a way out. At night, we have passionate sex. Nicky's mouth and hands on my body are the only things keeping me sane.

Later that night, we fall asleep, exhausted from making love, in a tangle of arms and legs and bare skin. Viktor's gruff voice startles me out of unconsciousness. I think it's a nightmare until his cold hand grips my shoulder. "Up," he growls. "Now." I'm instantly wide awake. The sheets are cool and empty next to me.

"Where's Nicky?" All of my spidey senses are tingling.

Viktor grunts a noncommittal response and gestures toward the door. I rub the sleep from my eyes, drag my fingers through my hair, and try to maintain my composure as we leave the mansion and walk to the guesthouse. My guts clench, knowing what must inevitably come next.

"I thought Valentina wasn't coming back until tomorrow." Fear turns my blood to ice. I can't go through this again. Every muscle in my body tenses, wanting to run, but there's nowhere to go. Not with Viktor behind me and armed goons tracking our movements.

"She changed her mind."

At the door to the guesthouse, I balk, unable to make myself enter this house of horrors. Viktor gives me a shove. I stumble over the threshold into the empty room. But it's not empty. Nicky is there, strapped to the chair, his chin resting against his chest. Luis sits on the workbench, swinging his legs and sipping a bottle of beer like he's at a frat party instead of a psychopath's torture chamber. Valentina stands beside him, one arm wrapped around her waist, the other holding a cigarette. My lunch rises up my throat.

"Ah, Calliope. So glad you could join us. How have you been?" Valentina greets me, gliding across the room in her graceful walk to brush the hair away from my face. She bends to kiss my cheek. I turn away in revulsion. "Ah, it's like that, is it?" She takes a puff off the filter then uses the cigarette to point at the empty chair across from Nicky. "Strap her in."

The room is empty except for the five of us. Nicky hasn't moved since I entered the room. I think he's unconscious. Seeing him helpless and restrained escalates my terror to new heights. Part of my brain—the innocent, vulnerable part—separates itself from this madness and floats outside my body to somewhere safe.

Valentina takes Luis's beer from him and splashes it in Nicky's face. He jerks awake, yanking at the leather straps. His eyes come into focus, falling on me. For the first time, I see fear in his gray eyes.

"I'm disappointed in you, Calliope." Valentina paces at our side, gesturing with her cigarette, leaving a trail of wispy smoke in her wake. "I trusted you with my beautiful home, and what do you do? You skulk around making mischief, fucking my whore, and trying to turn him against me."

I can't look at Nicky any longer. Instead, I train my gaze on the floor until her red high heels invade my line of sight. I try to speak, but nothing comes out. I clear my throat. "I was bored."

Her laughter echoes in the empty room. "Oh, dear. You are so entertaining." With the ends of her talon-like fingernails, she caresses my bare shoulder. "Perhaps you will join me in my bedroom tonight. What do you think, Luis? Would you like to play with Calliope?"

"Sure," he replies, lifting his shoulder in a nonchalant shrug.

"What did you do to Nicky?" I ask, concerned by the way his head bobs like he's fighting to stay alert.

"No more than he deserved, the insolent whore." The sickening twist of her mouth gives her a maniacal air. She cocks her head, gaze brightening. "Aw, you care for him, don't you? How sweet." She throws the cigarette to the concrete and grinds out the stub with her stiletto. "But he's not worth your pity. Men seldom are."

"He needs a doctor." The paleness of his complexion scares me.

"He'll be fine." The tone of her voice is a combination of amusement and cruelty. "I know my methods are a bit eccentric, but I think we had a very informative session tonight. You see, I learned some very interesting things while I was gone." Digging her fingers into Nicky's thick hair, she yanks his head back. "Didn't I, darling?"

Whatever she's done to him isn't visible from the outside. There's no blood. No bruises. No rips in his clothing. Maybe he's drugged.

He drags his tongue over dry, cracked lips. "Go fuck yourself."

"Tsk, tsk. That's no way to talk to the woman who holds your life in her hands." Her shoes click on the floor as she walks to Luis. Anticipating her needs, he withdraws a cigarette from a silver holder, places it between her lips, and lights the tip. He's nothing more than a trained pet to her. She caresses his cheek.

"Thank you, sweet boy." Pivoting on her heel, she returns to Nicky's side. "Tell Calliope what I learned about you yesterday." Her flat black eyes study me. "You see, he's a terrible person. Tell her about Milada, Nikolay." When he doesn't react fast enough, Viktor grabs my hand and begins to bend one of my fingers backward.

"Don't talk, Nicky." I squirm, trying to escape Viktor's grasp, terrified beyond measure. As much as I fear the pain, I can't bear to see Nicky cave to her demands.

Nicky's chest rises and falls with a labored breath, like he's weighing the punishment for noncompliance. "She's my daughter."

"Yes!" Valentina claps her hands together. "That wasn't so difficult, was it? Now tell her why."

"Because I fucked my brother's fiancée." His words are thick, slurred, untidy. My heart breaks for him. At the same time, I feel a mixture of relief and gratitude when Viktor releases my hand.

"Isn't this fascinating?" She rests a hip against the arm of Nicky's chair. Her entire body vibrates with excitement. "It's like a Russian soap opera. The younger brother has a secret baby with his brother's bride-to-be. The older brother raises the child as his own. Nikolay abandons the girl, going about his life, whoring and partying without a care in the world. I love it." A chill runs down my back when her attention returns to me. "And you'll never guess what I learned about you."

"I'm breathless with anticipation," I reply dryly. All

the while, I scan Nicky's face, willing him to look at me, to give me a sign that he's okay.

"I learned that you have a sister—a very pretty, younger sister." A sharp pain slices through my chest like I've been impaled. She taps her glossy lips with a fingertip. "Jagger, I think. I can hardly wait to get my hands on her. A pair of Jones girls should fetch a handsome price on the underground market."

"I'm going to kill you," I growl, fighting against the restrains.

"Have you figured out why you're here yet?" she asks.

"I have no idea, but leave Jagger out of it. I'll do anything you ask. Anything." And I will. I'll grovel, beg, and play her sadistic games for the rest of my life to save my little sister. More than ever, I understand Nicky's dedication to this psychopath. He had no choice. Just like me.

"Since you're having trouble remembering, let me help you out. It was about six years ago. You and your colleague removed several valuable paintings from my villa in Rome."

The blood drains from my head into my toes, leaving me dizzy. I remember all too well what happened. Cash had assured us it would be a simple job. The owners were out of the country. Loco, one of Cash's men, had gone with me. We were to get in and get out with the paintings. But something had gone wrong. Someone was home and interrupted us in the middle of the heist. Loco had shot down the man who confronted us. He was really more of a boy, not more than twenty years old. The event had haunted me for years. His senseless killing had persuaded me to leave the business for good. And for six long years, I'd plotted and planned and saved up my money, waiting for an opportunity to leave.

"I remember. It was an accident."

"You gunned down my son in cold blood." Her red lips part in a smear. "He was the light of my life, and you killed him."

"It wasn't me. It was Loco. I didn't know he had a gun until it went off."

"Loco said it was all your fault." Her thick eyelashes lower. With her thumb, she flicks ashes onto my bare legs.

"He's a liar."

"I know. That's why I killed him." The click of her heels as she moves around the room echoes in my head. She halts in front of me again. "After my precious boy's funeral, I swore to find the people responsible for his death. I had a hell of a time finding you, but now, here you are." Her tone is conversational, pleasant.

"What do you want from me?"

"I want you to suffer as I have suffered." The hardness to her oval face is more frightening than the most gruesome horror movie villain. "Luis, come here."

The young man hops off the workbench and walks toward her. His stride is confident, almost cocky. He stops beside her. She gives him a long, lingering kiss. I watch, confused, as he crumples at the knees and falls to the floor. A dark pool of red spreads beneath him. She hands the knife to Viktor, the same one she uses to cut up her fruit at breakfast, and bends to look me in the eye. Her face is so close to mine that I can feel the puff of her breath against my cheek. "You *will* fear me, and when the time comes, you'll beg for me to end your life."

FOURTEEN

Nicky

The next time I open my eyes, I'm in bed. The room is dark except for bright moonlight streaming in through the open French doors. Calliope sits in a chair next to me. Her hair swirls around her head in a cloud of black ringlets. A slight breeze ruffles the hem of her sarong. Bruises dot her bare legs and midriff. She shifts forward to take my hand in hers. The firm grasp of her fingers chisels a crack in the wall around my heart. Memories of last night come rushing back. The endless questions. And the ugly truth about Milada.

No one knows but Roman. The guilt and shame have eaten at me for sixteen long years. Now my greatest sin has been laid at the feet of Valentina. She'll use the secret to torment me for the rest of my life.

"Don't move." Calliope strokes my cheek with the back of her hand. "You need to rest."

"No. I'm okay." Pain shoots through my body as I

swing my feet to the floor. The room spins as the blood drains from my head. "How long have I been asleep?"

"Two days."

Two days? "That can't be right." I press a hand to my temple then scan her for injuries.

"Viktor gave us some kind of injection. I just woke up about an hour ago." She nods toward a tray of food on the table. "Pablo said he's been checking in on us."

"What about you?" Worries for myself dissipate. Her soft brown eyes stare back at me. My insides melt. She's so strong. So beautiful. "Did she hurt you?"

"I'm okay." Her fingers slip from my grasp as she reclines in the chair. She turns away, watching the tide ebb and flow on the beach. "But Luis isn't."

An insistent pain stabs between my eyes. I swallow down a lump of disgust and regret. No one deserved to die like that. Not even Luis. "She's totally lost it."

"I know." Tears well in her eyes. I can't bear the sight. I pull her onto my lap and wrap my arms around her, ignoring the pain in my ribs. She buries her nose in my neck. "She threatened Jagger. What if she finds her? I'll die before I let that happen."

"Where is she? Is she safe?" I stroke a hand through her hair, wanting to provide comfort. She doesn't deserve this. If only I could snap my fingers and make this all go away.

"I don't know. I think so." Turning misty eyes to meet mine, she musters a tiny smile. "She has money, and she knows how to hide better than I do."

"Well, if Valentina knew where she was, she'd

already have her here." Calliope wraps her arms around my neck and presses a kiss to my jaw. "And where is the bitch today?"

"I don't know." Her embrace tightens. "Just hold me, Nicky. I'm so scared."

"Me, too." I wish I had words to take away her fear, but I don't want to lie to her. We're in a bad situation that can only get worse. Instead, I hold her close, savoring the press of her breasts against my chest, her warmth, the beat of her heart. She's real and the only thing holding me together in the midst of this shitshow.

"Don't take this the wrong way, but I'm glad you're here," she whispers, so quietly I almost miss her words. The confession means more to me than anything.

All my life, I've kept women at arm's length, enjoying their bodies while numbing my heart to any meaningful connection. Not this time. In a matter of days, Calliope has worked her way into the shadowy corners of my soul. I hold her tighter, press a kiss to her temple, and reply, "Back atcha, Jones."

FIFTEEN

Calliope

Valentina is gone all day, but her absence does little to ease my anxieties. Every second is spent dreading her return. Nicky does his best to distract me. We discuss ways to survive this horror. Each conversation ends with the same revelation. If we want to live, we have to escape.

Once the sun sets, Viktor takes Nicky away. Hours later, he hasn't returned. Worry churns the contents of my stomach. Whatever he's going through isn't pleasant. I sit on the bed, too anxious to sleep. My pulse races, knowing I'm next. I don't know if I can endure more of her twisted torture. My mind races through dozens of different scenarios. Every encounter with her escalates in intensity. She's unraveling and we're the lucky recipients of her insanity.

There's a knock on the door. My blood pressure skyrockets. *No, no, no. I can't do this. I'm not ready.*

Viktor unlocks the door. He's carrying a dress, shoes, and a tiny black thong and throws them at me. "Put these on. Make yourself nice. You have ten minutes to meet me in the hallway."

"Why?" I shrink toward the headboard, unable to stop the trembling of my legs.

"Boss Lady is having a party and wants you to attend."

Terror turns my insides to ice. Undoubtedly, I'm part of the entertainment. If this is anything like my first night here, it's going to be painful. I need to stall. "I thought she was away on business."

"She was, and now she's back." He walks into the hallway and closes the door behind him.

I thought I had more time to shore up the emotional walls inside my head. Maybe this is part of her game—building expectations then shattering them. I pull on the dress, if it could be called that. It reminds me of my days on the stage. The tops of my breasts spill over the tight spandex material. The short hem reveals the cheeks of my ass. I drag the straps of sky-high stripper heels over my feet.

Viktor opens the door. His gaze sweeps over me, filled with heat. The walls of my throat constrict, making it hard to breathe. "Downstairs. Let's go."

As I walk down the sweeping staircase, I can feel his lustful gaze on my behind. After I kill Valentina, he's next on my list. We pass through a set of double doors into an enormous ballroom. Colored lights illuminate the chair on a stage at the opposite end. Men in tuxedos and women in expensive gowns chatter in conversation. Nicky is nowhere to be seen. The guests turn in unison to look at me. I must be a sight in my slutty apparel.

"Ah, here she is. My new toy. Isn't she lovely?" Valentina sweeps forward, her long hair swinging with each step. She hooks her arm through my elbow. "Come, Calliope. I want you to meet my guests." We push through the crowd. "Look at her. Isn't she magnificent?" she purrs to a short, bald man with too many rings on his thick fingers.

"Beautiful. Such lovely skin." He smooths a hand over my arm. I recoil at his clammy touch. "How much?"

"Patience." Valentina gives his hand a playful smack. "First, my toy is going to dance for us. We can talk price later."

Bile rises in my throat. Is this her latest ploy? I'm not sure what she means, but I have a feeling it has something to do with the stage at the end of the room. We continue our circuit of the room. Every step is agony. I've been here before. Years ago. Forced to entertain my stepfather's friends and bar patrons. Time never erased the pain of being objectified by strangers. I have no idea how she knows how much I hate this, but she does. By the smirk on her red lips, she glories in my discomfort. Some of the men touch my hair, my breasts, my ass. And there's nothing I can do to stop them.

At the front of the room, she climbs the platform

steps, dragging me with her. I want to object, but the moisture has left my mouth. The lights dim until we're standing beneath the spotlight. Sultry music pumps through the hidden speakers. Thank goodness I haven't eaten since breakfast because I want to vomit. Right here on the stage.

"No," I whisper, finding my voice again.

"Oh, yes." Using her little finger, she brushes the hair back from my temple. "Dance for me, my pretty. And make it good, or I'll show you pain like you've never known."

"I can't."

"You will." She tilts my face up to hers. The flat coldness in her gaze carries a hint of demented delight. "I insist." With a tiny shove, she propels me toward the chair.

"Please. I'll do anything. Not this." When Cash rescued me from the strip club, I swore I would never dance again. Yet, here I am, once again a puppet in someone else's show.

"Our girl is feeling shy." Turning toward the guests, she calls out, "Do I have a volunteer?" A murmur ripples across the floor. The short, bald man shoots a hand into the air. Valentina makes a show of surveying the crowd. Nicky is standing at the back of the room, partially hidden in shadow. She claps her hands. "Nikolay. Won't you do the honors?"

I don't know if I'm relieved or mortified. His gaze avoids mine as he climbs the stairs. Viktor stands a few feet away, hands clasped in front of him. The air thickens until I can hardly breathe. A dozen faces stare expectantly at me. Valentina presses Nicky into the chair. A muscle ticks below his cheekbone. I rub sweaty palms over my thighs.

"I won't do it." My voice is louder this time, more confident.

In a flash of movement, Valentina snatches the hair at the back of my head, bending me backward, exposing my throat. The gesture forces me to look in her eyes. "Viktor, take her to the guesthouse."

"No. Wait." I swallow down my objections. It's only a dance. One dance. I can do this. Anything to avoid the chamber of horrors.

"Excellent." A sickening grin curves her red lips. She presses a kiss to my mouth then releases me. I stumble back a few steps before regaining my balance on the tall heels.

The music grows louder. The song changes. I close my eyes, blow out a cleansing breath, and try to find the beat. It's a familiar song, my signature song when I headlined at The Twisted Garter. The bass thumps. I used to love dancing, before it became shameful. My head bobs and my hips begin to sway. One foot in front of the other. *Baby steps, Calliope.* I run my fingers through my hair, bend over slightly and swing my hair from one side to the other. When I straighten, Nicky is staring straight at me. Anger brightens the color of his eyes, but there's more than fury. There's lust and heat and need.

So, I dance for him and only him, blotting out the

balding fuck at the edge of the stage and the other perverts drooling in the audience. I put everything I've got into grinding on Nicky's lap, smoothing my hands down his legs, writhing against his chest. He's hard within seconds. Knowing he's turned on by my shame is empowering and filthy and serves to prove how fucked up I am. He becomes my anchor in a sea of rage and embarrassment and lust, because I'm just as turned on as he is.

"Take it off." Valentina tucks a Ben Franklin into my cleavage.

The song is extended play and seems to go on forever. Fuck it. This moment doesn't define who I am. I'm a victim of her debauchery and nothing more. I won't let her break me. With my resolve bolstered, I grab the hem of my dress, drag it over my head, and continue dancing. When the music ends, I'm out of breath and left standing in the center of the stage, naked, staring out at a sea of strangers. Humiliation rushes in to replace my defiance. It's only been about ten minutes, but it seems like a lifetime.

I'm so going to kill her.

"Good girl." Valentina pats my ass like I'm an obedient puppy. "You did amazing, my pet. Since you behaved, I'm going to give you the rest of the night off. Viktor, take her back to her room." In this moment, I'm flooded with conflicting emotions—relief, disgust, gratitude. I reach for my dress, eager to cover my nudity. She kicks the garment aside, out of my reach. "Leave it."

I'm forced to walk ahead of Viktor. I hold my head high, refusing to show a morsel of embarrassment, but once the bedroom door shuts behind me, I break. My knees buckle. I sink to the middle of the fluffy rug and let the tears flow. A few minutes later, the door creaks open. Nicky pulls me into his arms, brushing my hair away from my face.

"Hush. It's okay. You're okay." He murmurs the words against my ear.

"No. It's not okay. It's fucked up." I shove against his embrace, desperate to isolate myself. Too many feelings rush through me at once. More than I can handle. I dangle on the edge of no return, ready to shatter into a thousand pieces.

"I know, baby. I know." Instead of releasing me, he scoops me up and carries me to the bed. He strips out of his shirt and wraps it around me, somehow knowing that I need a physical barrier between me and the outside world. Then I'm sitting on his lap, back in his arms. I bury my face in his neck. The tattered remnants of my self-respect lie in shambles at our feet.

"How did she know?" The tears slow. I swipe at my cheeks and lean back to look up into his face.

"Preying on your vulnerabilities is what gets her off." His lips brush my temple. "I think that's what she does when she's gone. She's investigating our histories to find our weaknesses."

"Well, she hit the jackpot. When I was fifteen, my mom moved us in with her boyfriend Ben. She went through a lot of men, but Ben was a pretty nice guy. He owned a strip club. We lived in his apartment upstairs. He bought me clothes and picked me up from school. It was nice to have a father figure around for a change. Then Mom got arrested for drugs and went into rehab for the hundredth time. I could either stay with Ben or go into the system.

"Once she was gone, everything changed. Ben said I needed to pull my weight, pay for rent. I looked a lot older than my age. So, he put me on the stage, dancing. He'd have private parties for his VIP customers. They paid a lot of money for private dances. Extra if they could put their hands on me.

"Mom came home, but nothing changed. By this time, I was featuring at other clubs, making decent money, but he kept all of it for himself. I hated her for not protecting me. And I was terrified he'd do the same thing to Jagger. I was trapped with no way out until Cash came along."

I expect to see pity or disgust on his face, but there's neither. He takes my chin in his hand, tilts my face to his, and presses a light kiss to my forehead. "You did what you had to do to survive. There's no shame in that."

His words give me a little solace. My life has been a series of hard choices. As a fifteen-year-old girl with no money, no home, and low self-esteem, I did the best I could. Thank goodness, Grandma kept Jagger with her. My sister's life might not have been idyllic, but at least she didn't have to deal with our stepfather and the strip club.

When the lights are out and we're in bed, I crawl into Nicky's arms. I need to feel something besides the ache of humiliation and regret. Moonlight streams through the open French doors, giving the room an ethereal blue glow. We're far enough away from the party that the only sounds are the crashing waves and wind chimes.

I slide a hand along his sternum. His skin warms my palm. The solidity of his muscular torso provides an anchor in the hurricane of the night's events. I move closer, melding my body to his.

"Calliope." My name is a low growl in his throat. I silence him by touching my lips to his. He pulls back. "I don't want to take advantage of you when you're feeling like this."

"Just shut up and kiss me." I slide my hands around to his ass and dig my fingers into his hard muscles. The length of his cock presses against my bare stomach. Reaching between us, I guide him inside me. This isn't about sex. This is so much more. I need to feel a connection to a flesh-and-blood human being. Someone who isn't interested in ripping out my soul.

We move together slowly, too weak and tired for more than that. He's saving me from the chaos in my head. I hope my body does the same for him. His fingers entwine with mine. Strength and comfort flow between us. I know it's crazy, but there's nowhere I'd rather be at this moment. If I ever get out of this mess, I won't forget him. Nicky Tarnovsky will haunt my dreams for the rest of my life.

Afterward, I'm able to sleep for a short time in the security of Nicky's arms because I've come to a decision. Valentina knows about Jagger. She'll never be safe. I don't know how or when, but before I draw my last breath, Valentina Sokolov is going to die.

SIXTEEN

Calliope

Midmorning of the next day, Viktor arrives in our room. Nicky and I have been sitting on the veranda, staring numbly at the sea. "Valentina wants to see you." Both of us rise to our feet. "Not you." He shakes his head at Nicky and points to me. "You."

My stomach twists into an anxious knot. The emotional wound of last night has receded but hasn't disappeared. I wipe sweaty palms on my lap. Nicky stands. "I'm coming, too."

"Let's not make this a big deal." Vik pats the bulge in his pants pocket, alluding to the gun he always carries.

"It's okay." I extend a hand. He has no idea of my plan, and I want to keep it that way. Maybe he can go on to live a life after this.

With each step closer to Valentina, my pulse rate climbs. I have no idea what she wants, but I'm sure it won't be pleasant. The walls protecting my dignity have been shattered because of that bitch. Viktor opens the door to a theater room and steps aside for me to enter. A movie screen covers the far wall. Plush recliners rest on risers.

Valentina sits on a sofa at the back and pats the cushion next to her. "Come here, lovely. Sit by me."

Every fiber in my body resists. My feet are frozen to the floor. Viktor gives my shoulder a shove. I stumble forward and perch on the edge of the sofa. Valentina smooths a hand over my hair, pushing the unruly strands away from my face. Her touch is gentle and terrifying.

"You did so well last night. Such a beautiful girl. My friends were thrilled with your performance. Mr. Haskell offered fifty thousand dollars for you." She caresses the side of my face. Bile rises in my throat. This is even worse than I thought. "And when I showed him this video, he upped his offer to one hundred thousand."

With a click of the remote control at her side, a pornographic movie starts on the screen. The volume is too loud, filling the room with the moans and groans of the couple in front of the camera. Heat rushes into my face. I know the man's voice. It's Nicky. I bite my lower lip to temper my reaction. Then I realize the woman in the video is me.

"What?" The word slips out of my mouth before I can stop it.

I can't stop staring at the screen. It's us in the camera. The slap of skin on skin rings in my ears.

Valentina mutes the volume. I try to avert my eyes, but she takes my chin and forces my gaze to the screen. "No. Watch. You're amazing. So passionate, don't you think?"

"You taped us?" I don't know why anything she does surprises me. Still, I'm shocked and sickened. "How?" I searched every inch of the room for cameras.

"Oh, yes." With another click of the remote, she skips to last night. Tears sting my eyes. "He's a great lover, isn't he? So tender with you. He was never like that with me—or the others." A final click of the button displays a montage of Nicky with other women. Dozens. The sick twist of Valentina's smile tells me everything I need to know.

"You're disgusting."

"Oh, yes. I pride myself on it." Her laughter rings through the room. "Don't be angry. You were magnificent. And Nicky—he did exactly as I told him. Such a good little whore." She pats my hand. I shrink away from her touch. "How do you think I knew about your sister? You spilled your guts to him, and he told me everything."

It takes a few seconds for the meaning behind her words to sink in. I don't want to believe what she's saying. "I don't understand."

"I thought it would be amusing to have him seduce you, and I was right. You were so easy. Practically throwing yourself at him." The shame from last night returns. How could I have been so stupid? I place a hand on my chest. It feels like my heart is being ripped into pieces. Triumph curves her mouth. “He likes it, you know? Being watched while he fucks other women. It turns him on.” A devious gleam brightens her dark eyes. “But don’t worry. You won’t have to deal with him any longer. I’ve decided to accept the offer of Mr. Haskill. He’ll be here to pick you up within the week.”

SEVENTEEN

Nicky

The second Calliope arrives at the table for lunch, I know something has happened. I can tell in the way her gaze avoids mine. The devastation in her eyes completes my hatred for Valentina. She's done something—something awful. I rise and pull out a chair for Calliope. "Are you all right?"

"Don't." Her reply arrives through gritted teeth. She's changed into a white and purple flowered sundress that flatters her golden skin.

"What has she done?" I press for an answer because I can't fix something I don't know about. The thought of losing her creates unbearable tightness in my chest.

"I showed her your glorious catalog of films. Poor darling was shocked." Valentina brushes the backs of her fingers over Calliope's cheek. She turns her head away from the caress. I can see how much she's hurting inside.

I want to explain, but I can't. Not in front of Valentina. Anything I say will be refuted by the traitorous viper. Judging from the hatred in Calliope's eyes, she's not open to the truth right now anyway. "Someday, Valentina, karma is going to bite you in the ass, and I hope I'm the one to give it a kickstart."

She fills her plate with fresh fruit and yogurt, ignoring my words. "You know, I'm growing bored with you, Nikolay. You're no fun anymore. I think it's time for you to go. We can call our bargain complete."

"Nothing would please me more." Except the thought of leaving Calliopc alone with this psychopath is more distressing than I realized. When I'm gone, there will be no one to protect her.

"Great. I'll make the arrangements." Valentina fills Calliope's plate, as well. "You have to eat, *querida*. I need you healthy and healed for Mr. Haskill."

The mention of the smarmy bald businessman turns my stomach. "What have you done?"

"I've found a home for Calliope. I was going to keep her, but I've got business to attend and no time to properly deal with her. He's made an amazing offer. She'll live out the rest of her days in luxury on his private island." A tiny smile curves her mouth. "At least what's left of it."

"You mean, he'll torture her to death." I jump to my feet and slam my hands on the table. "He's a sadist. You're handing her a death sentence. Haven't you made her suffer enough?"

The color drains from Calliope's face. Valentina

shrugs. "What do I care? She means nothing to me." Her too bright smile makes me want to vomit. While she speaks, she uses her knife to slice a papaya in half. "Good afternoon, Viktor. You're just in time. I was just telling Nicky I'd like him to leave today."

"I'll make the arrangements." He pulls out the empty chair next to Calliope. Valentina places the knife on the side of her plate. A flicker of fury flashes through Calliope's brown eyes. In a movement too fast to comprehend, she grabs the knife and plunges the blade into Vik's neck.

Viktor's eyes roll into the back of his head. He slumps forward in the chair, his forehead banging against the table. Blood soaks his shirt. Valentina stares at Vik in stunned horror. Calliope's chair falls backward, crashing to the concrete. She hesitates for a fraction of a second. Our eyes meet. Terror and absolute determination flash across her face. She yanks the knife out of Viktor and brandishes it toward Valentina.

The guards surge forward, guns pointing at Calliope's head. I step between her and two of the soldiers. For a tense moment, the only thing I can hear is the pounding of my heart in my ears, the rush of blood through my veins, and the harsh rasp of our breathing. I raise my hands, trying to diffuse the situation as best I can. "Wait. Easy. Calliope, drop the knife."

"No." Like her voice, the tip of the knife trembles. "I won't be sold to some sadistic freak. You can kill me right now. This ends today."

"Everyone, calm down." Valentina's tone is low and

soothing. She extends her palms toward her men like she's wielding an invisible forcefield to hold them back. "I don't want her hurt." She edges toward Calliope. "Give me the knife."

"I'll die before I spend one more day here." Calliope backs toward the pool.

"Calliope, look at me." I force calmness into my voice. Her liquid gaze flits to mine. "This isn't helping matters. There's nowhere you can go. Drop the knife."

"I trusted you, but you're just as bad as they are." Her declaration wounds me to the core.

"I know. I'm a horrible person, but I'm on your side, and I always have been." I take a step toward her. "Please." The soldiers move their guns from Calliope to me. I don't care. All I can think about is minimizing this crazy cluster fuck before we're both killed. I lower my voice so she's the only one who can hear me. "Live to fight another day."

Valentina lunges for her. One of the soldiers presses the muzzle of his rifle against my temple. Another aims at my chest. The women topple to the ground. They roll around, grunting and cursing. Valentina grabs the knife and slashes Calliope's arm. Valentina is taller, but Calliope is stronger. She delivers a punch to Valentina's throat that knocks her on her ass. The knife splashes into the pool.

Victory is short-lived. The soldiers converge on Calliope. She's dragged from the patio, kicking and screaming, fighting to her last breath. Valentina struggles to her feet. The pristine white of her blouse is dotted with her own blood. She uses a shaking hand to brush the hair away from her face. "You'll pay for this, Calliope Jones."

"Wait. I'll make a new bargain with you. My life for hers." The soldiers force me to my knees.

"I'm done with you," Valentina replies, pivots, and heads toward the house.

One of the soldiers raises the butt of his rifle. Colors explode inside my head and everything goes dark.

EIGHTEEN

Nicky

When I open my eyes, blurry overhead lights blind me. The room comes into focus. Beige walls. The smell of antiseptic. The low hum of voices. Roman steps into view. Rourke hovers behind him. Lines of gravity etch their faces.

"Welcome back." A doctor wearing blue scrubs speaks in stilted English. "How are you feeling?" As she speaks, she shines a tiny flashlight in my eyes.

I lift a hand to my head, trying to ease the infernal ache between my temples. "Like I've been run over by a truck."

"You have a concussion and two broken ribs." She raises an index finger in front of me and moves it from left to right. I follow the motion with my eyes, wincing at the stabbing pain caused by the action. Her serious expression holds kindness. "You're going to have a headache for a few days."

When she leaves, Roman drags a chair to my bedside. "You look like shit."

"That explains a lot about how I feel." Slowly, I turn my head to face him.

"Somebody beat the crap out of you. A farmer found you in the middle of the jungle. If he hadn't come along, you probably would have died out there." The annoyance in his tone has a familiar ring. "Would you like to explain what you were doing in Colombia?"

Fragments of memories collide. Calliope. Viktor. Valentina's threats. I bolt to a sitting position. Sharp needles stab my side. "Milada? Is she okay?"

"She's fine. She's on my island with Claudette. We were on my yacht with Henry and Everly heading to meet them when we got the call about you." He leans back in his chair, brow furrowing.

My relief at knowing she's safe is short-lived. "I have to go back."

"What's going on, Nicky? Talk to me."

"Valentina. She's been holding me captive at her compound. She threatened Milada."

Roman's blue eyes darken. He leans forward. "And you're just now telling me about this?" Fury thins his lips. "What have you done?"

"Everything you asked." His highhandedness ignites my own anger. The words stick in my throat. Breathing becomes difficult. I swallow and lean back on the pillows. Nothing I say will change his mind about me. The only thing that matters right now is Calliope. I tug the IV from my arm, swing my legs over the bed. The room tilts.

"Whoa. Nicky, you need to stay in bed." Rourke places a gentle hand on my forearm.

"You don't understand." I push her hand away.

"Are you crazy?" Roman rises to his feet.

"Why do you have to go back?" She gazes up into my face. For the first time, her blue eyes hold concern instead of animosity.

"Because Calliope's still there, and I can't leave her with that psycho bitch." I have no idea how to make them understand the urgency of the situation.

"Calliope?" Roman narrows his eyes.

"A woman. Valentina plans to sell her to someone." Frustration swells inside me until I feel the walls of my chest expand. "I don't have time for this."

"Roman, look at him. He's telling the truth." Rourke places a hand on her husband's arm. Her gaze is both tender and stern. He draws in a deep breath. The connection between them is palpable. I don't know why I couldn't see it before. They love each other. She touches his face, an unspoken conversation passing between them. "He's family. You owe him this."

Roman traces a fingertip along the curve of her jaw before turning his dark blue gaze on me. I stare back, willing him to see my sincerity. He steps between me and the door. "You can't go back there alone. Tell me what you need, and I'll make it happen."

NINETEEN

Calliope

After the incident with Viktor, Valentina's minions dragged me by the hair into a nearby utility shed and locked the door. I'm pretty sure I broke her nose during our struggle. Serves her right. The next time, she won't walk away. The wound in my arm has stopped bleeding. I rip the bottom from my sundress to fashion a makeshift bandage. It's unbearably hot in the small space. Sweat trickles between my breasts. I squeeze my eyes shut and rest my head against the wall. Images of Nicky keep flashing on the backs of my eyelids. The blow to his head had been ferocious. Her goons hauled him away. Tears thicken the walls of my throat. If he isn't dead, he will be soon.

I search the shed frantically for a way out. My fingers ache from clawing at the dirt floor, but my chest hurts even more. The thought of Nicky fills me with unbearable despair. Now that I've had some time to think, I'm not so sure he betrayed me. Valentina has a way of twisting facts into fantasy. I have no idea what to believe. All I know is that without him, I would have died on the first day. He endured Viktor's abuse to protect me. No one would do that. He deserves the benefit of my doubt.

The sun sets and takes the warmth with it. I hug my knees to my chest in a desperate effort to drive away the chill. I've been in here for hours. Dehydration cracks the skin on my lips. After a while, exhaustion takes over. My chin hits my chest, and I doze. The next time I open my eyes, it's daylight again.

No one comes for me, which is both a blessing and a curse. The closed space acts as an oven, intensifying the tropical heat. Now that the adrenalin has faded from my system, I can feel each of the numerous scrapes and bruises on my body. Insects crawl over my skin. The mosquitos are terrible. To pass the time and keep my spirits up, I visualize a different life for myself—one filled with laughter and smiles and—Nicky? His presence in my fantasy is unexpected but welcome. I'd give anything to see his mischievous smile, to hear his deep voice and feel the crush of his lips against mine.

When night comes back around, my arm begins to throb and feels hot to the touch. Infection is a real threat in these unsanitary conditions. I'm no doctor, but I know enough to be concerned. I'm more worried about dehydration. A person can live for days without food, but in this heat, I won't make it long without water.

Relief comes on the third day when the door creaks open. Two soldiers motion for me to step into the bright sunshine. My legs wobble. I'm too weak to walk. One of the men hoists me over his shoulder and carries me to the house. He drops me onto the green grass next to the pool. Valentina stands on the patio near the French doors. Purple and green bruises surround her eyes. A bandage covers her nose. The sight raises my spirits. No matter what happens to me, she'll never forget who did that to her.

She approaches, keeping a healthy distance from me. "Haskill is waiting for you at the dock. I hope you suffer through every second of the rest of your short, miserable life." I flinch as she spits at my bare feet.

"You'll burn in hell for this," I shout as the soldier scoops me into his arms. At the Jeep, my wrists are ziptied together and I'm dumped into the back seat. One of the soldiers sits behind the wheel. The other climbs into the back with me.

My heart pounds against my ribs. I'm too weak to fight. The infection in my arm aches. Fever dulls my reflexes. This is my only chance for escape. Once I'm on a boat, I have zero chance at finding freedom. I lift my head to scan the thick jungle as we jolt down the dirt track. Even if the vehicle slows down, I don't have the strength to run. And as Nicky said, there's nowhere to go.

So, this is it. I watch the tree branches overhead, savoring the patches of blue sky and the smell of saltwater. Feverish images float through my head—my mom, Jagger, Gran. For the first time since my arrival, all hope leaves me.

No birds sing. The only sounds are the Jeep's engine and the wind through the trees. Four pops like firecrackers come from the direction of the compound. The spray of machine gun fire follows. The driver stops the vehicle. Both men shoulder their guns. I lift onto an elbow. That's when I see them. A group of men wearing camouflage step out of the brush. They point their weapons at my captors. Both soldiers drop their weapons.

"You take care of them." I recognize the deep male voice. Unshed tears burn my eyes. I don't have enough moisture left in my body to cry. His voice is closer now. "Calliope?"

His dark head peers over the side of the Jeep. I lick my lips, fighting for the strength to speak. "I'm here."

"I've got you," he says, his voice tender. Strong, gentle arms lift me up. Relief washes through me before the world fades away.

"Hello. How are you feeling?" The beautiful redhead stares down at me, her blue eyes wide with concern. "Henry, she's awake." A regal blonde man peers over her shoulder at me.

"I'll let the doctor know." Henry's voice holds notes of command and strength which are more comforting than frightening. He disappears from my sight as his footsteps fade into the distance.

I struggle to an elbow, ready to defend myself,

although this woman seems harmless. My trust in humans, however, has been decimated. Something else Valentina stole from me. From the gentle rocking motion and the sea beyond the window, I'm on some kind of boat. Haskill's boat? Panic replaces the blissfulness of sleep. "Where am I?"

The redhead pats my hand. "It's okay. You're safe." Kindness warms her smile. "I'm Everly, and that was my husband Henry. We're Nicky's friends. You're on a yacht in the Caribbean with Roman Menshikov and his wife Rourke."

"Nicky? Is he here?" A rush of warmth flows through my body. He came back for me. At the lowest point in my life, he didn't abandon me. "I need to see him."

"He's here. He hasn't left your side for the past twenty-four hours. I promised to sit with you while he took a shower." She presses back on my shoulder. "Just rest. Henry will get him. You need to stay put for a bit. The wound on your arm needed stitches. You were dehydrated and had a terrible fever when you got here. The ship's doctor says you're going to be fine."

Now that my faculties are returning, the bag of saline comes into focus, hanging from a hook above my head, and I feel the pull of the IV taped to my opposite hand. "Valentina, where is she?" I'll never feel safe, not until I know she's six feet under.

"She can't hurt you." The sound of Nicky's voice causes my heart to ping against my ribs. Bruises splotch his face, and he moves slowly, like he's sore. Despite the injuries, he's still got a regal presence, his movements graceful. Gratitude tightens the walls of my throat. He risked everything to save me.

Everly rises from her chair, pausing to squeeze Nicky's shoulder on the way out the door. "I'll give you some privacy."

The doctor arrives and checks my pulse, removes the IV, and assures me that my wounds are superficial. After he leaves, an awkward silence fills the room. I have so many questions, so many things I need to say to Nicky, but I have no idea where to start. He sits in the chair next to my bed, crossing an ankle over the opposite knee in a casual pose, but his leg bounces like he's nervous.

"Well, it's not every day you get the Queen of Androvia as your nurse. You should feel honored." His gray eyes are soft, like finely spun wool. They bore into me, baring my soul. For the first time in my life, I feel *seen*.

"That was the Queen?" I push myself up on the bed. "For real?" Her face *had* seemed familiar. "A regular nurse would've been just fine."

"Not on Roman Menshikov's boat." Nicky's laughter lessens the tension between us. I drink in every inch of his face, happy to see him away from the gloom of the compound. We've only known each other for a few weeks, but it feels like a lifetime. "I thought you were dead. Are you okay?" Tears of relief prickle behind my eyelids.

"Nothing time won't heal." He places both feet on

the floor and leans in to take my hand, one of the few places not bruised on my body.

"Are you sure about Valentina?" I want to believe him, but my faith in people has been shaken to the core.

"You need proof." As always, he understands what I need before I ask. The pad of his thumb strokes my palm. I've missed him so much. "I have her. She's not going anywhere."

"You came back for me." My voice breaks. I bury my face in my hands to hide the waterworks pouring out of me.

"Shhh…it's okay. You're safe. It's over." In a flash, I'm enveloped in the safe haven of his arms, my face buried in the crook of his neck. His fingers caress the curve of my back, steady and reassuring, the same way they did on our first night together. He smells familiar, like soap and expensive cologne, the best scents in the world.

"I thought you were dead." I cling to him. My fingers dig into his back until he grunts in pain. "Oh, I'm sorry." I try to back away, to give him space, but he tightens his embrace.

"No worries." Then he says the most wonderful words in the world. "Don't let go."

TWENTY

Calliope

The next day, Everly teases apart the tangles in my freshly washed, curly hair and pins the locks on top of my head. Intense concentration furrows her pale brow. Her red hair is pulled into a high, messy bun that compliments her oval face. The hem of her pale blue maxi dress swirls around her silver sandals as she works.

"I feel a little weird having my hair done by a queen," I say. My reflection in the mirror shows an unfamiliar woman with a thin face and shadows under her eyes. Two days in the shed sapped my strength. Makeup hides the worst of my bruises. The doctor gave me something to sleep last night, but I'm exhausted—physically and emotionally. My fever is gone, and the wound in my arm aches a little less. On the outside, I've begun to heal, but I have a feeling that on the inside, I'll never be the same again.

"Oh, please. I do my own hair every day." Everly waves a hand. Her warm, friendly smile seems sincere.

"Unless she has a formal function, and then she has a team of minions to do her work." Rourke appears in the doorway holding an armload of apparel. This is my first day out of bed, and at her invitation, I'm having dinner with the guests. I'm nervous about meeting her husband, the eccentric billionaire who funded my rescue. His reputation as a hard ass doesn't help my anxiety.

"People expect a certain amount of pageantry from the royal family." Everly winces as she tugs on a stubborn snarl like the pain is hers instead of mine. "Don't let her fool you, Calliope. She has just as many people at her beck and call as I do. Maybe more."

"Fair enough." Rourke shrugs, and with a guilty smile, drops the clothes on the bed. "I think these should fit you. What do you think?" She spreads a variety of shorts, pants, and sundresses over the dark blue comforter.

"I like the white dress with the crisscross straps," Everly offers. "It will look great against your tan."

The two women have been pampering and fawning over me since I woke up. Their kindness and concern surpass anything I've experienced in my twenty-eight years. Everly brought me tea and sandwiches on a silver tray, even though there are stewards onboard to do those things. Rourke ran a hot herbal bath and, since we're of similar size, provided clothing to replace the grimy sundress I'd been wearing. Despite their generosity, we share a sense of wariness. They don't know me. And I'm too broken to trust anyone.

"I like the yellow one." Rourke holds up the dress to me. She's pretty in a normal way, not at all like a billionaire's wife. Sun-streaked dark blonde hair skims her shoulders when she moves. I try not to gasp at the exorbitant price tag hanging from the strap. She chuckles. "I know. The prices still shock me, too."

Tentatively, I touch the dress. "I like this one." The airy cotton glides through my fingertips. "It's beautiful."

"Excellent choice." Rourke smirks at Everly. The queen rolls her eyes but smiles like she enjoys the teasing. Their relationship is easy and effortless, something I envy. I've never had a female friend. Never cared to. Watching them makes me wonder if I've missed out.

"Have you known each other long?" I ask, curious to learn more about them.

"We met when we were kids. Our parents were friends." Rourke sits on the bed, her blue eyes earnest. "My parents died when I was young, and I had to go live with my aunt. They left me penniless. Life was a real struggle, but Everly's family supported me through all of it. I don't think I would have survived without her." They share a glance of mutual appreciation.

Everly takes Rourke's hand in hers. "I know I don't tell you often enough, but I love you." When her eyes meet mine, they sparkle with tears. "Our lives might look wonderful on the outside, but we've gone through a lot of terrible things together. She's been my rock."

"You're lucky to have someone." Watching them

reminds me that I have no one waiting for my return. If I had died at Valentina's hands, no one would have looked for me. The knowledge hurts more than I could have guessed. I want what they have. Caring friends, loving husbands, a family.

"Oh, don't get me wrong. We've had some killer fights." Rourke rises from the bed to wrap an arm around Everly's shoulders. "Especially over Nicky. He almost tore us apart."

My ears perk at the mention of his name. A weird pain stabs my heart. "You were together?"

"For a short time," Everly says, a guilty blush staining her high cheekbones. "Well, as much as anyone can date Nicky." He had a relationship with this gorgeous creature? There's no way I can compare to her long legs, radiant complexion, and cascading auburn hair. Sensing my unease, she backpedals quickly. "It was no big deal. Just a fling to get over my divorce."

"Thank goodness you came to your senses. He's not the kind of guy to lose your head over," Rourke adds. "But I'm sure you've figured that out about him, Calliope. It only takes a minute to realize he's a playboy through and through."

"Sure." I bite my lower lip and turn back to the array of clothing to hide my emotions from her. Of course, he's had a life outside of Valentina's compound. He's too handsome and too rich and too charismatic to live like a monk. My thoughts bounce back to the dozens of videos in Valentina's library and the pain of seeing him with all those women. I swallow, trying to regain my composure. On the other hand, the pull of attraction between us is undeniable. Deep down, I accept that he could never have real feelings for me. I'm a high school dropout, former prostitute, and a thief. Sometime soon, we're going to part ways, and I'm going to have to admit the truth. We're nothing to each other, only strangers brought together by a shared experience.

"Hey, things are getting a bit heavy in here, don't you think?" Everly clears her throat and forces a bright smile. "We're celebrating tonight."

On legs still shaky from my ordeal, I stand. Rourke lowers the dress over my head. Everly tugs the seams and straps into place. The airy fabric floats over my curves. The hem falls just above my knees. The tight bodice boosts my ample breasts up to impressive heights. Simple yet stunning. I smooth my hands down my stomach, noticing with approval that I've lost a few pounds.

"You look amazing. But you need something more." Everly unclasps the thin gold chain from her neck and drapes it around mine. "There. That's better, don't you think?"

"Yes. Perfect." Rourke presses her hands together, blue eyes sparkling. "Yellow is Nicky's favorite color. He's going to die when he sees you."

The mention of his name brings a rush of heat into my face. I want him to feel the way I do; excited, nervous, hopeful. Before the emotions get out of control, I shut them down. This is the end of our journey together, and I need to prepare for my exit.

"Look. She's blushing. It's so cute." Everly bites her lower lip to contain her amusement. "Have you two—I mean—did you—?"

"Everly!" Rourke rolls her eyes, interrupting the queen before she can continue. "Even if they did—you know, do the deed—it's not our business."

"He's got a huge dick," Everly replies, ignoring her friend. "No one will blame you if you did."

"Stop it." Rourke turns me toward the mirror and nudges a loose lock back into my updo.

"Thank you so much for all that you've done. You've both been so nice to me. I don't know what to say." I try to maneuver the topic of conversation away from my obvious crush on Nicky to something less personal, but I hope they're right about the dress. With my curls tamed and hints of mascara and blush, I've been transformed from a wayward wreck into a normal person, almost unrecognizable from the Ohio bartender. Aside from the bandage on my arm and the haunted shadows in my gaze, no one would suspect what I've been through.

"It's been our pleasure," Rourke replies. "We're just happy to have another female around to cut some of the testosterone on this boat."

Everly adjusts the shoulder straps of the dress for the tenth time. "But for the record, I've been nicer, right?" Her tone carries unbridled mischief. "I mean, if you had to make a call, it would be me, wouldn't it?"

"Whoa. Hold up a sec." Rourke raises her hands, joining in the fun. Her diamond and sapphire wedding ring gleams in the sun slanting through the cabin windows. In my previous life, I would've snatched the ring from her finger at the first opportunity. Not now. I've changed in ways I never expected. Her eyes crinkle at the corners. "It's really unfair to put Calliope in a position like that." She hooks her arm through my elbow, leading me toward the door, then bends to whisper in a conspiratorial tone. "But if you had to pick, it would be me, right?"

For the first time in weeks, laughter bubbles up my throat. It's great to feel something other than anxiety and pain. We leave Rourke's master suite and walk down the corridor past warm wood paneling, priceless paintings, and sumptuous leather furnishings. In my head, I tally up the value of each item, unable to stop the old habit. On the next deck, the dining room table is set for dinner. A warm breeze blows in through the open windows. The walls, the floors, the furnishings—all are pristine white and contrast with the brilliant azure of the Caribbean Sea. It's the first time I've been beyond my cabin since arriving. I pause, letting the salt air caress my face. Freedom has never felt so sweet.

The men are gathered at the stern, smoking cigars and sipping whisky. Their deep rumbling voices quiet upon our entrance as if they sensed our presence before we arrived. Henry steps forward, takes Everly's hand in his, and bends to place a kiss on the back. "My queen."

"Oh, stop." Everly rolls her eyes, but a blush turns her ivory skin to a bright rose. Her embarrassed gaze slants to mine. "He's showing off to impress you."

"Calliope, we haven't been properly introduced. Henry Von Stratton. It's an honor to have you with us. Nicky has nothing but wonderful things to say about you." Henry releases his wife's hand to take mine. His grasp is warm and strong.

"Thank you. It's an honor to meet you, Your Majesty." I'm not sure if I should bow or curtsy, so I do an awkward combination of both, stumbling a little in the process.

"Oh, no. Everly is right, as always. None of that here. This is one of the few places in the world where we can be regular people." A British accent adds to his regal persona. His cool blonde handsomeness is the perfect foil to Everly's fiery hair and personality. "And you must call me Henry."

"All right." The power of their presence overwhelms my composure until Roman steps forward.

"Calliope, welcome. I'm Roman Menshikov." He's the tallest person in the room. Inky black hair curls above his collar and a sprinkling of afternoon shadow covers his square jaw. He's wearing board shorts and deck shoes. The unbuttoned front of his white shirt reveals a dusting of chest hair over rippling abs. Like the royal couple, he bears an aura of command.

"Thank you for having me. Your boat is lovely." We shake hands. His dark eyes search mine. I'm not sure what he's looking for, but I have a nagging feeling that I don't measure up to his high standards.

"It's a yacht. Don't call it a boat. He gets very angry about that." Nicky's lips brush my earlobe as one of his arms steals around my waist. He crept behind me so quietly that I didn't hear him approach. My skin pebbles at his nearness, especially knowing this could be one of our last moments together.

"Only because you treat it like a fishing boat every time you borrow it." Roman's gaze cuts to his younger brother. Their dynamic bears traces of animosity on both sides. In just a few words, I can sense the tension between them.

Nicky shrugs. When he removes his arm, I shiver at the trail of his fingertips over my ribcage. He faces me, straightening the collar of his linen shirt, letting his focus linger on my breasts and legs. One corner of his mouth curls upward. I've missed that sinful smile and all the dirty, sexy things it promises.

"Roman, be nice. You promised." Rourke steps between us to button up her husband's shirt. Her tone is half-amused, half-chastising.

"I am." His gaze follows her fingers along the placket. "This *is* nice—for me."

"No. You're not. Bring it down a notch, would you? Don't be a dick." She's unfazed by his penetrating stare. Not only is she nice, she's brave for holding her own against this imposing man. "Aren't you going to change clothes for dinner?"

"Nope." The tenderness in his touch as he brushes her hair away from her face contrasts with his gruff demeanor.

"Heathen." She shakes her head, but her eyes are filled with affection.

"My boat. My rules." As he watches his wife adjust his clothing, the hardness on his lean face melts into adoration. "I'll do better."

She rises on tiptoe. Presses a kiss to his mouth. "Thank you." With a final pat to his shirt, she gives me a reassuring smile. "His bark is worse than his bite. Most of the time."

"Why don't we sit down? I think dinner is ready." Roman sweeps a hand toward the dining area.

After the meal and pleasant conversation, we move to the stern. The sun has set, leaving a deep blue sky sprinkled with stars. The quiet hum of the engines and rush of water provide soothing background music to the evening. Nicky stands at the railing, cocktail in hand, his gaze never wandering from me. Having him near soothes the lingering anxiety created by Valentina's mind games. Memories of her are never far from my thoughts, snaking tendrils of malice through my brain. Even though the weather is balmy, I shiver.

"Here." Nicky drapes an arm around my shoulders. His warmth chases away the internal chill. Rourke and Everly exchange glances. Although we're removed from the other couples, I'm conscious of their constant appraisal. The weight of their gazes reminds me that I'm not one of them. The uber wealthy. The chill returns.

"Thanks." I curl into his embrace. Our eyes meet. His returning smile goes straight to the space between my legs. A hunger unfurls in my center, one that won't be satisfied by anything but his lips on mine.

"If you're up to it, could we chat for a minute?"

Roman stalks toward us, directing the question to me. He eases onto one of the white sofas and gestures toward the matching sofa across from him. With a flick of his fingers, he dismisses the stewards. They file out silently, leaving us alone with the hum of the engines and the lapping of water against the hull.

"Um, sure." Reluctantly, I leave the security of Nicky's side and take a seat in the chair across from his brother. A nervous sweat dampens my palms. I feel the same way I did when the high school principal caught me smoking in the restroom. Nicky leans against the deck railing a few feet away.

"I suppose you have questions." Roman speaks around the cigar clenched between his teeth.

"Yes, sir. Many." I don't know why he intimidates me. Maybe it's because I robbed his guests at the Masquerade de Marquis. Shame and guilt persuade me to lower my gaze. As if he senses my distress, Nicky takes a seat beside me. The lean solidity of his thigh presses against mine.

Roman leans forward to open the laptop on the coffee table between us. "What I'm about to tell you is confidential and must never leave this yacht. Do we have an understanding?" As he talks, he taps on the keyboard.

"Yes." I nod and curl my fingers into fists, trying to prepare myself for the surprises ahead.

He turns the laptop around to face me and scrolls through a series of drone photos. "This is Valentina's compound, or what's left of it." A charred pile of ash, broken beams, and cement foundations litter the ground where the house once stood. The tropical paradise is now a decimated war zone. I stare at the wreckage, waiting for relief, finding none, and hating her for it. "She's been a blight to the underground for a decade. I've tolerated her because she's been useful to me in the past, but after what Nicky told me about her depravity, I had no problems using my resources to take her out."

He swivels the laptop screen to face him and types in a few more commands before turning it back to me. My stomach twists. This time, it's a live video of Valentina in some kind of small white cell. I gasp. A shudder shakes my shoulders. She paces back and forth in front of a cot, her movements hindered by shackles and handcuffs. Her hair is ratted, her face bruised and swollen from the broken nose I gave her.

Nicky slides his fingers through mine. "Don't worry. She can't get to you."

"Where—" My voice cracks. The walls of my throat are dry, like I haven't spoken in years instead of minutes. "Where is she?" I cling to Nicky's hand, drawing strength from his touch.

"Downstairs in the hold. I have a guard outside her door. She can't escape." Roman leans back, resting an ankle on the opposite knee. Tendrils of smoke curl around his head. "Now, the question is—what do you want me to do with her?"

"Me?" I lick my parched lips and glance at Nicky. "You're asking *me*?"

He nods, pulling my hand onto the top of his thigh.

His gaze holds mine. Truth and reassurance soften his eyes. "In my family, justice is a personal matter. When someone wrongs us, we deal with it on our own terms."

"Well—" I stare at the broken woman in the live feed. Her agitated pacing reminds me of a caged tiger. Memories come flooding back. The abuse. The torture. The psychological scheming. Her threats against Jagger, Milada, and the death of poor Luis. Anger builds in my blood, rising from a simmer to a boil. She's evil incarnate. This time when I answer, my voice is confident, strong. "What are my options?"

"We have a few choices." Roman nods like he understands, and maybe he does. According to Nicky, his family was executed by insurgents. He understands revenge as well or better than most people. "She has many enemies in the drug world who would love to have her. The CIA, DEA, and FBI are eager to make an example out of her before the next round of federal elections. We could give her over to any one of those groups."

"Personally, I think we should tie an anchor to her feet and drop her overboard," Nicky says. Hatred roughens his deep voice. His fingers tighten around mine. I glance up at him through my lashes. A muscle twitches above his jaw. The sight of Valentina affects him, too, reminding me that I'm only one of her many victims. She has to be punished. I squeeze his hand. Our eyes meet. His lips twitch into a humorless smile.

"I want her to suffer." It's an ugly confession, but

I've never claimed to be a good person. "I want her to dread each day. I want her to feel the way we did."

"Right. Well, there's a third option." Roman clears his throat and glances at Nicky. An unspoken conversation passes between the brothers, as if seeking and receiving permission to divulge a dark secret. "I have an acquaintance who runs a prison in Russia for people like her."

"Prison is too good for her." I've never felt this way before—so ugly inside, and I blame her for the intensity of my dark emotions.

"This isn't your ordinary facility," Nicky adds.

"No. The conditions are—rough. The most heinous of underground criminals are held there. They have only their most basic needs met. And the warden is, shall we say, unconventional. They use inmates for the testing of interrogation methods. She would be held in solitary confinement for the rest of her life. No human contact outside of the experiments. Nothing but concrete walls and silence."

Nicky releases my hand to pull up a website on the laptop. The facility is an ancient fortress on top of a desolate mountain surrounded by peaks of snow and ice. "This is hell on Earth."

"I'm not sure." I bite my lower lip. The wound on my arm stings. Every muscle in my body aches from Valentina's mistreatment. For the rest of my life, I'll carry her monogram on my hip. She's marked me for eternity, body and soul. I lift my eyes to Nicky. "What do you think?"

"This is your choice," he replies, brushing his thumb over the back of my hand.

"I was faced with the same kind of decision once." Everly steps forward, clinging to her husband's hand like he's a lifeline. Her voice reminds me that we're not alone in the room. "Before you make a choice, there are things to consider." A deep sadness clouds her features. "Right now, you're probably angry and hurt and itching for retribution. In time, those feelings will fade and change. Ten years from now, you might not be the same person you are today. The choice you make needs to be one you can live with. This is more about you than her. Being merciful isn't a weakness. It shows strength of character and the ability to break the chain of cruelty set forth by your enemy."

"Whatever you decide. No one will judge you." Rourke rubs a hand along Everly's back. "And no one outside this room will ever know."

Valentina stops pacing and turns to face the camera in her cell. Any traces of beauty have dissipated. There's no audio on the video. She opens her mouth in a silent scream. But her eyes are what get to me. They're still flat, black, and empty. Those vacant eyes remind me how it felt to be locked away with no hope of escape. A small glimmer of satisfaction begins to unfurl. "Can I have some time to think about it?"

"You have until morning," Roman replies. "We'll be landing at my private island tomorrow, and I want to finish this business so I can enjoy a little downtime with my family."

"That's very generous of you." I flick a glance at Nicky. His expression is smooth and unreadable. I'm not sure how he feels about the situation. "I'd like to talk to her."

"I don't think that's a good idea." Roman shakes his head, his hair brushing the collar of his shirt with the movement. He stands, takes the laptop from the table, and snaps the lid shut.

"She can handle herself," Nicky interjects. "If that's what you're worried about. She took out Viktor with a paring knife."

Roman stares at Nicky, eyes widening. "Is that so?" His words hold a grudging note of respect. "I always hated that bastard." Then he shrugs. "I'll have one of my men take you down there. But not tonight."

I don't think I can sleep knowing the devil is somewhere on this boat. Nicky voices my thoughts. "Tonight is better."

"Suit yourself." Roman tucks the laptop beneath his arm and heads toward his wife. He bends to kiss her. "No more work this evening. I promise."

"Good." She beams at him and brushes his hair away from his face.

"Thank you." Words seem inadequate for the rush of gratitude swelling inside me. "I don't know how I can ever repay you. Especially after what I've done."

"There is something." His ominous tone brings a feeling of dread along with it. I turn to face him. His dark eyes meet mine. "Nicky tells me that you're an expert at breaking and entering. We recently had a breach of security at my England estate. I'd like to sit down with you sometime and discuss ways to prevent something like this from happening again."

Roman doesn't know that I was the one to rob his manor house. My gaze flits to Nicky. His eyebrow twitches, but his face remains expressionless. He didn't tell on me, another debt to be repaid. I place my hand over his and squeeze.

"Sure. I'd be happy to help you in any way I can." It's the least I can do in light of recent events. In time, I'll tell him the truth, but not now. Not tonight.

"And while you're here, I'd appreciate it if you stay in your cabin unless accompanied by one of us." The gravity of the lines bracketing Roman's mouth make my stomach twist.

"What the fuck, Roman?" Cold fury turns Nicky's chiseled features into the frightening man who followed me home from the bar. "She's been chained up in a garden shed for two days. The last thing she needs is to be locked up again. Have a little compassion."

"Roman, I think you're—" Rourke jumps into the conversation but is silenced by her husband's raised hand.

"We don't know this woman. Not really. Until I have a thorough background on her, I'm obligated to protect us." Although his words make sense, shame washes through me. This is another example of how I don't belong in this world. "How much do you know about her, anyway, Nicky? I mean, truly know? You've been acquainted for all of what? Three weeks?"

"That seems a little harsh," Henry comments.

"I know enough. She's the bravest, most intelligent woman I've ever met." Nicky inches forward until he's nose-to-nose with his brother. "She did what she had to do in order to survive. Something you should relate with." The two of them glare at each other, a study in masculine hostility. "I won't stand by and see you treat her like a prisoner when she's been a victim from the very start."

"You have to admit, Nicky, that you've never been a good judge of character. If it was up to you, we'd have a boatload of prostitutes and strippers onboard tonight." Another wave of shame shakes my self-confidence. In Roman's eyes, I'm worthless.

"I remember a time when you loved a boatload of hookers," Nicky replies. Testosterone thickens the air. Everly and Rourke exchange worried glances. Henry frowns.

"You don't have to defend me, Nicky." The anger and frustration over Valentina's mistreatment come tumbling out, and it's all directed at Roman. "For your information, Mr. Menshikov, *I* was a stripper and a prostitute." I refuse to continue feeling shame for my past. "Not by choice, but because my pedophile stepfather forced me into it." Danger flashes in Roman's dark eyes. I keep talking because I'm done being intimidated by rich fucks like him. "When someone holds a gun to your head, the lines between wrong and right tend to get blurry. Not that I'm excusing anything I've done. I'll be the first to admit that my poor choices led me to those situations. I can only hope to do better in the future. But I won't apologize for who I am."

"Careful." Roman lifts an eyebrow in warning. "You have no idea who you're dealing with."

"I don't care if you're the King of fucking England." My voice grows louder with each word. I curl my fingers into fists, desperate to control my fury. Tears burn my eyes. I place a hand over my heart. "I'm not a piece of trash. You might not think so, but it's true."

Nicky wraps his arms around me. I bury my nose in his chest, fighting to halt the sobs building inside. "You're worth a million in my book." His hand strokes my hair. The brush of his lips tickles the top of my head. "Sweet girl."

Stunned silence blankets the yacht. I focus on my breathing. In through the nose. Out through the mouth. I'm so close to coming unhinged. Valentina would be thrilled to learn I'm broken beyond repair. Maybe forever.

"Are you finished?" A muscle twitches in Roman's cheek.

"Yes." My pulse settles back to a normal rhythm. I refuse to apologize for the outburst, but I need to make them understand, for my sake as well as Nicky's. "Wait. No, I'm not done." Passion vibrates in my voice. "You have no idea what that psychopathic bitch put us through. What she put *him* through." I place a hand on Nicky's cheek. He stares down at me, his gray eyes soft, filled with tenderness. "He endured tortures that will give me nightmares for the rest of my life. To keep all of you safe." I make eye contact with each person, starting with Everly and ending with Roman. "He sacrificed his self-respect, his dignity, his body—" Reviewing his actions tightens my throat to the point of pain. "For *you.* And you're treating him like he's a fool. Maybe you need to take a long look in the mirror, because he seems like twice the man you are right now."

Roman stares at me. I stare back, lifting my chin, daring him to say one more insulting thing. The seconds drag past. When I don't blink, the tension drains from his expression. He sighs and sinks into the nearest barstool. "You're right."

Rourke's eyes widen. Something like a smirk twists Nicky's lips. Henry and Everly don't even try to hide their smiles. I'm not sure why they're so amused, because I'm pissed beyond measure.

"I apologize, Ms. Jones. I've had a gun held to my head a time or two, and it truly does make morality seem dispensable." His fingers tap on the back of the couch. "As for Nicky, I've known him a lot longer than you."

"People change. Especially when they're faced with adversity. Maybe you need to stop seeing him as the person he was and start recognizing the man he is today." My gaze flicks to Nicky. His gray eyes watch me with an intensity that makes my heart skip a beat. "Because he's a hero to me, and I'll forever be grateful to him."

"I had no idea what you've done, Nicky." Everly's voice is thick with emotion.

"You should have told us." Rourke's forehead crumples, like she's about to cry.

The unplanned expenditure of emotion has sapped the last of my strength. I exhale, needing to be alone and collect my thoughts. "If you'll excuse me, I'm not feeling well." Part of the weakness in my knees is from the freedom of expressing myself after so much time at the mercy of someone else's whims. The rest is from Nicky's stare. I don't care what the others think of me. Just him. No matter what happens next, at least he'll know how much I appreciate him. I turn toward the exit.

"Wow. She told you, mate," Henry says to Roman, applauding. "Nicky, that girl is a keeper."

TWENTY-ONE

Nicky

Calliope disappears into the hallway. I stare after her, dumbstruck by her words. A hero? Me? The implausibility is comical. Roman's furrowed brow suggests he doesn't believe it for a minute, and Rourke's open mouth reinforces my assumption. The only person to entertain the idea places a hand on my shoulder.

"Is it true?" Everly's large eyes brim with tears. "You put up with that bitch for years to protect us?" I stare at the moonlight sparkling on the water, unable to meet her gaze, and shrug. "Thank you. So much. I'll never be able to repay you." She wraps her arms around me, holding me close. I hug her back, surprised by the way her embrace affects me. In my ear, she whispers, "I always knew you had a good man inside you."

"Damn it, Nicky. Let go of my wife." Henry's tone holds equal notes of warning and humor. He wraps an arm around the both of us. "If you don't go get that girl of yours, I'm going to do it, and then I'll have to make polygamy legal in Androvia."

I don't need to be told twice. I jog to the hallway. A glimpse of yellow catches my eye. Calliope's standing next to the railing, her dress rippling in the breeze. Her face is upturned, eyes closed, like she's praying to the silver moon overhead.

"You're not going to jump, are you?" I ask in a feeble attempt at humor. "Because that would be a terrible waste of time and resources."

Slowly, her eyes open. Her gaze meets mine. A jolt of desire hits me low in the gut, followed by a tug of empathy. I've never felt so much, so quickly, for anyone. Exhaustion and pain swim in her brown eyes. "By now, you should know me better than that."

"I do. It was a joke. A lame one." I lean an elbow on the railing and face her. "That was quite a speech you made. I think Roman's ears will be on fire for the rest of the night."

"They treat you like you're some kind of joke, and you're not." Her fingertips glide along the side of my face. I turn into her palm, savoring the sweetness of her touch. "You're an amazing man."

"I don't give a fuck what they think of me. I gave up on earning their respect years ago." Taking her hand in mine, I press a kiss to the inside of her wrist.

"But I do. I care. Everyone needs to know how wonderful you are." The softness in her eyes heats my chest. "I'll defend you until the very end."

I believe her. For the first time in my life, someone

values me for more than my good looks or my skills between the sheets. The amazing thing? She knows every horrible thing I've done, the sins I've committed, and the lies I've told. Yet, she still likes me. "You're a remarkable woman, Calliope Jones."

I continue dropping kisses along the inside of her forearm, her elbow. Every touch of my lips elicits a hitch in her breath. When I reach her bicep, I straighten and wrap an arm around her waist to pull her close. Her hair smells like coconut. My attention dips to her mouth, the full lips, her slightly crooked bottom teeth. I've never seen a more perfect woman in my entire life.

Her arms steal around my neck. I want to kiss her more than anything, but it will have to wait because Roman has followed us to the lower deck. Rourke holds his left hand. He braces the other hand on the railing and stares out over the water. Too much has happened between us. We'll never repair the wounds in our relationship.

"I'm sorry for interrupting, but we need to clear the air, once and for all." Roman's dark stare finds mine. "About us. About Milada." The only sounds are the thundering of my heart and the occasional cry of a seagull. We've never had a proper discussion about our shared daughter or the circumstances of her birth. He shoves a hand through his unruly hair. "I'm grateful for what you've done, and it's hard for me to admit that you've grown up. When you gave up Milada, you trusted me to take care of the most precious gift a man can receive. I never hated you for that. I only hate the way you pretended she didn't exist."

"I was seventeen and angry at the way my future had been sacrificed for you." Years of bottled up frustration bubble beneath the surface of my calm façade. "Do you know what happened to me while you were learning about royal protocol and dating debutantes, partying on yachts and being worshipped by every single person in your sphere? I was sent to military camp. Where I learned how to lie, cheat, steal, and kill. All so I could protect your sorry ass." The repressed memories flood my head. I rub two fingers along my temple to ease the burgeoning migraine. "I was eight years old, Roman. That was my childhood. No one asked what I wanted or who I wanted to become. My life never belonged to me. I made the sacrifices while you reaped the benefits of my unhappiness."

Roman is silent for a long time. The weight of his penetrating stare cuts into my heart. I wish I had a glass of scotch to numb the ache. After a dozen heartbeats, his gaze softens. "I'm sorry. I didn't know."

"Because you never asked." Back then, he'd been my idol. The adopted older brother whom I admired. He taught me how to skateboard and swim and ride a bicycle. He'd been larger than life to a little boy. The hurt from the past revitalizes. Inside me, that scared and broken kid still exists. "Didn't you ever wonder where I was?"

"They said you were at a different private school. I had no reason to question what they told me." The rasp in his voice suggests a pain I'd never considered. "You're forgetting that I had no choice either."

Calliope's fingers tighten around mine. Once again, she's the only thing holding me together. "You never seemed grateful. Not a single thank you. Just condemnation and ridicule and expectations."

"You were always so damn arrogant and spiteful," he says, his voice raw with emotions of his own.

"Because I felt out of control." The pain of being invisible grows as I free my pent-up anger. "You were the most important person in my life, and you never cared enough to notice how unhappy I was."

"That's not fair." Roman's voice grows in volume as his emotions bubble to the surface. "I took care of you. I paid for your college, your clothes, your fancy cars. I gave you everything you needed."

"Everything but my independence and your attention." I don't want to face my feelings, but it's too late to turn back. "When Claudette came along, I was so angry with you. I wanted to hurt you, and sleeping with her seemed like the fastest way. The only way to get your attention was to act out. I was seventeen. Only a few years older than Milada. I had no idea how impactful the consequences of my actions would become."

"You left me to clean up your mess. Again." He releases Rourke's hand and scrubs both hands through his hair until it stands up in disarray. "Do you have any idea how tired I am of always being the responsible one?"

“I know. I get it. I owe you a debt that I can never repay.” The admission almost guts me. There it is—the confession I’ve been too proud to say. “You’ve done a great job with Milada.”

“She means everything to me.” His deep voice cracks. “I’m grateful for her every damn day.”

“You both love her. She’s so lucky.” Rourke’s gaze softens when her attention returns to me. A few months ago, I would’ve killed for a look like that from her. It still means a lot, but not nearly as much as Calliope’s grip on my hand. “I’ll admit that your shenanigans make me crazy, but I had no idea you were so young when Milada was born. You were right to step back. You did the right thing, Nicky, and I’m sorry for judging you without knowing all the facts.”

“I’d like to have more of a relationship with her.” The words are difficult to say. I’ve spent a lifetime in denial about my daughter.

“She’s a handful.” Roman sighs. “I could use all the help I can get.”

“She tried to blackmail me for a Porsche.” The memory of it sparks a chuckle in my chest.

Roman stares at me then bursts into laughter. “She’s just like you. Stubborn. Willful. Devious.” A rare smile bows his lips. “Of course, she’s going to need to be told. Let’s make a game plan. We can tell her together after we dock.”

“I’d like that.” Emotion tightens my throat. Calliope rubs her thumb over the back of my hand. Roman shoves my shoulder playfully. It's as close to physical affection as either of us can stomach.

"I feel like we need a group hug," Rourke interjects. Tears glimmer in her eyes. Roman spreads his arms to encompass my shoulder and Rourke's waist. I drag Calliope along with me. The four of us stand in silence.

"Why are we hugging?" Everly steals up behind us to throw her arms around us. "We heard shouting and wanted to make sure no one was being murdered."

Henry stands next to his wife, shaking his head. "I'm glad to see someone else's family is as fucked up as mine," he mutters.

"I'm working on that." Everly lifts on tiptoe to kiss his cheek.

Roman extends his hand to me. "Truce? Can we start over?"

I take his hand in mine, feeling hope and strength in his grasp. "I'd like that."

TWENTY-TWO

Calliope

Roman leads us down the stairs to the lowest deck of the boat. Sweat trickles down my back, between my breasts, more from anxiety than the oppressive humidity. In the background, the quiet hum of the engines can be heard. The guard unholsters his weapon while Roman unlocks the door to Valentina's room. Of course, a Russian mafia prince has a jail cell in the underbelly of his yacht. My heart thuds against my ribs. I don't want to do this, but I have to.

Nicky stands at my back, his hand on my hip. He bends, his lips close to my ear. "Are you sure about this?"

"Yes." The rush of blood to my head from his heated breath leaves me dizzy.

"Ready?" Roman asks.

I nod. The door swings open. Roman, Nicky, and the guard flank the door. Four stewards block the stairs.

Valentina sits on the edge of her cot but springs to her feet at the sight of us. "What is going on? I demand to see the captain of this ship." Her words are clipped, almost hysterical.

"That would be me." Roman's voice is calm, cold. "And I have nothing to say to you." He steps aside to let me pass. "But Ms. Jones does."

Valentina's flat stare darkens at the sight of me and Nicky at my shoulder. "You." She almost spits the word. "Are you responsible for this? I should have killed you both when I had the chance."

Seeing her disheveled and broken bolsters my confidence. That's when it hits me. She can't hurt me anymore. Her words have no power. I lift my chin and return her glare. "You tried to break us and failed."

"When I get out of here, I won't make the same mistake twice." Spittle punctuates the force of her words. She brushes her tangled hair away from her face, a pitiful attempt at maintaining her previous persona.

"That's the thing. You're never getting out of here. You're going to a cold, dark prison in Siberia to live out the rest of your days in misery." Power fills my veins. I square my shoulders. She's not as tall as I remember. More fragile.

"My people will come for me." She laughs. The sound turns my stomach.

"Your people are all dead," Nicky says. He's still at my back, his chest pressing against my shoulder. Together, with Roman and his men, we form a formidable wall. "Your compound has been destroyed. You have nothing left."

"Yuri will be furious."

"I've reached out to Yuri, and we've come to an agreement." Roman's voice is calm and quiet, like he's discussing the latest football scores. "He's willing to overlook your capture in return for weapons and a new trade deal. I was surprised at how little he valued his wife's life. He seemed quite thrilled to assume control over what's left of your assets."

"No." In a fit of frustration, she bangs her fists on the wall. "I am the queen of Colombia. I'm powerful. You can't defeat me."

"No, Valentina." The softness of my tone echoes Roman's control. Seeing her anger and misery exorcises the last threads of the intricate web she had spun in my soul. This moment erases the damage she's done and replaces it with strength. "You are nothing."

At the door to my cabin, Nicky pauses. Standing next to him in the narrow corridor resurrects the attraction between us. He leans a shoulder against the wall, shoving his hands into the pockets of his trousers. His gaze locks onto my mouth. The gesture brings back memories of his kisses, the way he tastes like Macallan and cigars, the softness of his lips. I feel like a teenager on her first date.

"Well, you must be exhausted. You should get some

rest." With his little finger, he sweeps the hair away from my temple.

"Actually, I'm too wound up to sleep right now." Confronting Valentina lightened my soul. And the thought of leaving him is more than I can bear. Once he's gone, I'll have to face the emptiness of my future. "Do you want to come in?"

"I thought you'd never ask." A playful light brightens his eyes. He swings the door open and waits for me to pass. Once we're inside, he shuts the door. The room is small but luxurious with a queen-sized bed and two chairs. He takes a seat in the middle of the bed and pats the mattress in invitation. "Join me, Jones."

My heart thumps against my ribs. This is the first time we've been in each other's company without the weight of Valentina hanging between us. I press my trembling hands together. Roman was right. We barely know each other. One look at his beautiful face reverses that idea. I know him better than anyone. And he knows me. I ease onto the comforter at his side. "I think we need to clear the air about a few things."

"Okay." He licks his lips like he's nervous, then chuckles. "More sharing?"

"Those women in the videos, who were they?" I avoid his gaze and stare out the window at the bobbing horizon. "There were so many. I can't get the picture of you with them out of my head."

His hand finds mine and draws it onto his thigh. "Look at me, Jones." Reluctantly, I lift my focus to his. He tips my chin, using his forefinger. "Those women were her friends. She pimped me out at her parties. They meant nothing to me."

"She said you reported back to her. That you told her everything I said." I try to look away, but he holds me steady. "Did you do that?"

"No. Never. More of her lies. A part of her strategy to break you. To break us." The muscles in his throat work as he swallows. "After that first day, I couldn't betray you. You were so strong and defiant." His breath catches. The pad of his thumb sweeps over my lower lip. "I've never met anyone like you."

A wave of warmth creeps from my toes to the top of my head. Sincerity rings in his voice, his words, and shines in his eyes. I lift his hand to my lips and kiss his palm. His eyelids lower, hooding his eyes, but I can still see the heat in their depths. He leans forward and brushes a chaste kiss over my lips. When we part, the space between my legs aches for his touch.

"And what about Cash? Are you still—do you care for him?" He shifts, coming closer until his thigh brushes against mine.

"When I met Cash, I was desperate to escape the strip club and my stepdad." The memories are bitter-sweet. "At first, I was happy. He treated me well, bought me nice things, and taught me how to steal, but later, I realized that I'd traded one controlling man for another." A second, more unpleasant fact surfaces. "He's going to come looking for me."

"I'll take care of him."

"No." I swallow the lump in my throat. "You've

done enough for me. I'll be fine. If he was going to find me, he'd have already done it." Although, I'm not so sure. Cash has the patience of Job. For the rest of my life, I'll be looking over my shoulder, waiting for him to reappear. This, however, isn't Nicky's fight. It's mine, and I won't burden him with more of my bullshit

"And your sister? What about her? I could find her for you." His fingertips trail over the curve of my cheek.

My heart aches at the thought of my sister. "She's better off without me. I don't want to drag her into my drama. I made sure she was taken care of before I left her." With the money in my safe deposit box, she can go to college and create a bright future for herself. I'll miss her, but this is the best thing for her.

Nicky gives a heavy sigh. "I'd really like to seduce you right now, Jones, but we both need our rest."

As much as I yearn to have him inside me, the events of the day have sapped my strength. I lean my forehead against his, cupping his face. "Do you think you could stay with me until I fall asleep?"

I feel his smile. "It would be an honor."

TWENTY-THREE

Nicky

The next day, we disembark on Roman's island. I haven't been here in years. Not much has changed. It's interesting to see the place through Calliope's eyes. Seven timber and thatch huts span the edge of the white sand beach, each with a private pool. Gauzy white curtains flutter in the ocean breeze. The rooms are open and inviting, nothing like Valentina's ostentatious home. Her warm brown gaze bounces over the Jet Skis, the waterslides, and halts on the two figures walking toward us.

Milada skips over the sand, barefoot, and wearing a pink bikini. "Hey, Dad." My chest tightens. She breaks into a run toward Roman, reminding me again that I'm not her father. Not really. And never will be. Watching them hug, a different kind of emotion dissipates the envy. They love each other so much. My brother and my child. Maybe I've been looking at this from the wrong perspective.

"Is that Claudette? Her mother?" Calliope's hand, which had been firmly clasped in mine, falls to her side.

"Yes." I reclaim her hand.

Claudette trails behind her daughter, long and lean and toned in a fringed blue thong and matching halter top. Roman hugs Milada then Claudette. They've managed to forge a relationship, something I've failed to accomplish. We've been on-again off-again since Milada was born, hooking up whenever one of us needed sex, but I haven't seen her in a few years. Not since Valentina came into the picture. The shallowness of my actions fills me with shame. However, Claudette never wanted me. It was always about Roman for her. I was just a temporary distraction whenever she became bored or needed a way to manipulate his affections.

"She's really pretty," Calliope says, disappointment apparent in her tone.

"I suppose. If you like the tall, thin type," I reply. "Don't be intimidated. She has bunions, and her eyes are too far apart. Like a frog. And she farts in her sleep." Some of the tension in Calliope's grip eases away. I can tell she's fighting a smile by the way she tugs her lower lip between her teeth. "Personally, I prefer a little junk in the trunk." To demonstrate my preference, I wrap an arm around her waist and pull her into my side. A smile curves her bee stung lips. If I have my way, I'm going to spend some quality time alone with that mouth tonight.

"Nicky, hello. I had no idea you were coming." Claudette greets me in her French-accented English. She leans in to kiss both my cheeks. Her cool gaze lands on

Calliope. Judgment flickers in her eyes. "Where have you been, you naughty boy? It's been too long. I've missed you." Her hand lingers too long on my chest.

"Hello." I pull Calliope closer to me, moving away from Claudette's touch. "Claudette, I'd like you to meet Calliope. She'll be staying here tonight as my guest."

"Oh, I see." Her lids lower to hide her thoughts. She extends a hand to Calliope. "It's wonderful to meet you, Calliope."

"Thank you. It's nice to meet you, too." The two women shake hands. Calliope's smile is warm and accepting, despite Claudette's impudent stare.

Henry and Everly head to their accommodations for some alone time. Roman and Rourke follow Milada. The teenager halts in front of us, flipping sand all over my shoes. "Hey. I know you." She scrunches her nose at Calliope. "You're the girl in the handcuffs."

A deep red blush climbs up Calliope's neck and settles in her cheeks. To her credit, she recovers quickly. "Um, yeah. That was me. Nice to see you again."

Milada's attention flits back to me. Her ponytail swishes behind her. "My birthday is next week, Uncle Nicky, in case you've forgotten."

Seeing her healthy and whole is the best gift I've ever received. Everything I've done, the hell I've endured—it was worth it. "Really?" I arch an eyebrow, amused by her impudence.

"You're not getting a Porsche," Roman interjects.

Milada scowls, her gray gaze narrowing at me. "You told him?"

"He forced it out of me." I spread my hands in a gesture of surrender. "You know how he is."

"Great." The dramatic roll of her eyes causes everyone to laugh. "I already told all my friends."

"Well, you'll just have to untell them." Roman gives her a squeeze, hugging her into his chest and placing a kiss on the top of her head. "Now, let's all go up to the main house. We need to talk."

We gather around the long outdoor dining table. The staff deliver a tray of fresh fruit and cheeses. Milada and her mother sit across from me. Calliope's at my side. Beneath the table, her hand rests on my thigh. Having her here comforts me in ways I never expected. No matter what happens with Milada, Calliope will have my back. I brace myself for the worst possible scenarios. Tears, anger, or rejection. Possibly all three. And it's no more than I deserve.

Roman starts the conversation. "Milada, we need to have a conversation. I want you to listen with an open heart, okay?"

Her gray gaze bounces from her father to her stepmother and back again. "Am I in trouble? If it's about the police that night at Uncle Nicky's—"

"What police?" Roman's growls.

"No. There were no police." I shoot Milada a warning glare and wave my hands.

"What's going on?" Claudette's mouth presses into a tight line. "Shouldn't we discuss this first, in private? After all, she's my child, too."

"She needs to know the truth about us," Roman says. He jerks his head toward me. "All three of us."

Milada sucks her lower lip between her teeth. Her eyes narrow. I can practically hear the wheels turning in her head. "Is this about Uncle Nicky? Being my father? Because I already know about that." She reaches for a pineapple square and pops it into her mouth. "Mom told me a long time ago."

"You know?" My voice is higher than normal. Calliope's fingers dig into my thigh. "And you never said anything?"

"Why would I?" She shrugs then returns to the fruit plate for some papaya. "I'm not stupid. I've got a pretty good deal going."

Relief eases the tension I've been carrying around for the past sixteen years. Roman laughs, a hearty belly laugh, something I haven't heard from him in ages. Rourke smiles, too. Calliope bites her lower lip.

Claudette rolls her eyes. "Of course, I told her. She's too smart to hide things from. If I left it up to the two of you, she'd be in the dark forever."

"Are you okay?" Roman ignores Claudette, focusing his attention on Milada. "Do you have questions for us?"

"Not really." Milada shrugs, her ponytail swinging behind her.

"I'm sorry I wasn't around much while you were

small. It was in your best interest at the time." The confession is difficult. I clear my throat, trying to remain in control of the relief and gratitude growing in my chest. "But I'd like to spend more time with you in the future, if you don't mind."

"I don't mind." By now, she has a pile of food on her plate. "Will you teach me to drive? Mom can't drive. I'd ask Dad, but he yells too much."

I glance at Roman then Claudette, waiting for their input. They both nod. "If it's okay with your parents, I'd love that."

"Cool." She fidgets in the seat. "Can I go now?"

Roman nods. "Sure."

Milada takes her plate of food and skips off in the direction of the chef's teenaged son. The rest of us share a collective sigh of relief. I have a daughter. *A daughter.* I keep repeating the words in my head. No more lies. No more dark, dirty secret. The truth has set me free. Calliope smiles up at me like she can feel my happiness. For the first time in my life, I have a sense of hope for the future.

TWENTY-FOUR

Calliope

We spend the rest of the day sunning on the beach, sipping fruity drinks, and soaking in the peace of the island. Roman and Rourke wander off to snorkel. Nicky and Milada play frisbee in the sand and make plans to begin her driving lessons when they return to the city. Watching them together brings a smile to my face. Their laughter floats like music on the ocean breeze. They're so much alike. Nicky moves slowly, wincing now and then from the pain of his ribs, but he makes a valiant effort to keep her entertained. I love watching him like this, carefree and happy.

Sitting here with the wind ruffling my hair and the sand squishing between my bare toes, the horrors of the past weeks seem like a bad dream. My thoughts keep drifting to the future. I can't return to Ohio. Too much has changed. I'm not the same person that I was. A fly lands on my towel. I flick him away, filled with envy at his sense of purpose. I have no idea where I'll go or what to do with the rest of my life.

"How long have you been in love with him?" Claudette sits down beside me, stretching her tanned legs in front of us and crossing them at the ankles.

"Um, excuse me?" Her patronizing tone raises the hackles on the back of my neck.

"Nicky. You look at him with big puppy dog eyes." She tosses her shiny hair then leans back on her elbow, showing the taut stretch of her flat belly.

"It's not like that." But maybe it is. My attachment to him grows stronger with each passing day. And it's going to hurt like hell when we go our separate ways.

"I hope you like heartbreak, because Nicky is the master." With her eyes closed, she tilts her face to the sun. "He will reel you in, but when it's time to commit, he'll leave you like his feet are on fire." When I don't reply, she keeps talking. "He's so intelligent. Much too intelligent for someone like you. Don't be offended. It's just a fact. He's too smart for me, too. Half the time, I have no idea what he's talking about. Did you know he's the youngest person to pass the New York bar exam?" She cracks an eyelid to gauge my reaction then closes it with a satisfied smirk. "He'll never settle down, but if he does, it will be some high society woman with a giant bank account and big tits."

I don't say anything. Mostly because I don't owe her any explanations. And partly because I have a feeling she's right. A few yards away, he drags his shirt over his head and tosses it aside. He's an awesome display of rippling abs and biceps. His new beard lends his beautiful face a fierce edge. If I'm honest with myself, I want him in my life. I want to be the woman who holds his heart. He catches my gaze and smiles. The reaction jolts straight between my clenched thighs.

Later, we gather around the outdoor dining table for a shared meal. Roman, Nicky, and Henry tell amusing tales about their days in college. Their hearty laughter booms across the glassy surface of the swimming pool. Rourke and Everly talk about how they met their husbands. I listen, fascinated by the shared dynamics of these people. Although they argue and fuss, they seem like a real family, something I've never had, and the realization makes me sad. Maybe I should reconsider my solitary future.

Afterward, Nicky walks with me down the path to my bungalow. The tropical leaves cast flickering shadows in the torchlight. An air of comfortable awareness stretches between us. He holds my hand, his fingers threaded through mine. And I like it. I like it more than anything. When this ends, I'm going to be heartbroken.

"You've been awfully quiet." The sound of his voice resonates through me, deep and rich. "Are you okay?"

"Sure. Fine." I avoid his gaze as we climb the steps to our open-air bedroom. He halts outside the threshold.

"The helicopter will take us to the airport tomorrow. I'm flying back to Manhattan. Where would you like to go? I'll make the arrangements for you."

I should be eager to return to the real world, but I'm not. By now, I've been fired from my job. The thought of my empty apartment fills me with sadness. I have nothing and no one. No reason to return to Ohio. But isn't that what I wanted? The freedom to walk away from commitment and obligation? "Okay. Thanks." I tuck my hair behind my ear, glancing down at the floor, embarrassed by my circumstances. "I don't really have anywhere to go. Any suggestions?"

He rests his head against the doorjamb, staring down at me with an intensity that stirs butterflies in my belly. "New York City is a good place to start over."

"I suppose so." Suddenly, being around him makes me nervous. I rub my sweaty palms over my hips. If he looks closely, he'll see my angst, and I can't let him know about my silly crush. This isn't me. I'm tough. My heart is encased in steel, impervious to love and other pointless emotions. But not this time. Not with him. He's changed everything in the best possible ways.

He brushes the hair from my eyes. His fingertips sweep along my cheek, come to a rest beneath my chin, and tilt my face up to his. "Well, you should get some rest. I'll see you in the morning."

The bed is big and lonely without him in it. Before Valentina, I treasured my privacy and independence. I smooth a hand over the cool sheets, wishing Nicky were beside me with his big feet, hard body, and massive cock. I've fallen for him—hard. How is that possible? We've known each other less than a month. No one falls in love over three weeks of captivity. He's my kidnapper. I should hate him, but I don't. I'm in love with him.

In the morning, there are hugs and promises to keep

in touch from Rourke and Everly. Roman and Henry shake my hand. Milada hugs Nicky so hard that it causes a lump to form in my throat. He remains stoic as we board the helicopter and then Roman's private jet. He's silent the entire flight. *When it comes time to commit, he'll run like his feet are on fire.* Claudette's words echo in my head. Is that what he's doing? Pulling away?

While I pretend to read a magazine, he holds meetings and makes phone calls in an effort to catch up on his work. I watch him from beneath my lashes. As he talks to someone on his laptop, he rubs the backs of his fingers over his beard. Not so long ago, he caressed my bare skin the same way. A pulse of need makes my pussy clench. I shift positions, crossing and uncrossing my legs to lessen the ache. Sensing my stare, his gaze flicks up to mine. A flash of heat rises up my neck and settles in my face.

"How long until we land?" he asks the flight attendant.

"We'll begin our final descent in about fifteen minutes, sir." The flirtatious smile on her face suggests she finds him attractive. Of course, she does. His navy suit fits him to perfection. Our time in the sun gave his skin a bronzed glow. Streaks of gold highlight his dark brown hair. I'm jealous of every woman who ever touched him because he's mine. *Mine.*

Without another word, he closes his laptop, stands, and heads for me. My pulse climbs as the distance shrinks between us. When he reaches my side, he extends a hand. On instinct, I slide my palm over his. The glide of my skin against his makes my panties dampen. I follow him to the back.

We're in a bedroom. I only have a flash of luxurious bedding, neutral colors, before I'm pinned against the wall by his big body. He sweeps my hair over my shoulder and sucks the sensitive spot beneath my ear. His hands roam over my breasts and hips, dragging my shorts down to cup my pussy.

"I want you, Jones," he whispers in my ear. His breath burns my skin. "Open your legs for me."

"Hurry." I'm desperate to have him inside me one last time. I unzip his fly. He's hard and ready. His pulse echoes in the vein running along his shaft. I kick aside my clothes and wrap a leg over his hip. In one vicious jab, he's buried to the hilt. All the way. Every glorious inch of him.

He pounds into me. My back thumps against the door with each thrust. I don't care who hears my cries. Our harsh breathing fills the room. The slide and drag of his cock through my slick flesh brings me to the edge within minutes. I try to memorize every facet of him—the scent of his cologne, the grunts he makes, the silkiness of his hair in my clutching hands. When the landing gear touches down, those memories are all I'll have left of him. A tear rolls down my cheek at the exact instant my orgasm unfurls. Nicky drives deep inside me and shudders.

Someone knocks on the door. The flight attendant's

voice is inches away from my head. "Sir, we need you to take your seats, please."

"Be right there." Nicky's voice breaks. He rests his forehead against mine, chest heaving, his hands still clutching my hips.

I can't bear to look at him because this is it. The end of us. I'm not sure when he became a part of me. It happened so stealthily that I didn't notice until this very moment, and now it's too late.

He backs up, tucks himself away, and smooths his hair. I grab my clothes and shimmy into them, avoiding his gaze. A dozen heartbeats later, we're buckled into our seats on separate sides of the plane. The wheels skip and catch on the runway. This nightmare is over. I should be ecstatic, but I'm not. A sense of loss ruins everything.

A limousine waits on the tarmac. The driver opens the door. I hesitate. The longer I wait, the more painful this is going to be. I need to rip off the bandage. "Um, I can just catch a cab."

"Nonsense." With a hand on my back, Nicky nudges me forward.

"No. Really." I muster a weak smile. Black sunglasses obscure his gray eyes, but I can feel his gaze on me. I hold out a hand to shake. "Thank you for everything."

"How are you going to pay for a cab? You don't have any money." When he doesn't shake my offered hand, I let it drop to my side. An amused smirk twitches his lips. The ice in his gaze turns his gray irises to steel.

He's back to the cool, sardonic man I met at the bar last month. My captor. My savior. My love.

"I'll manage." I try to brush past him, but he steps in front of me.

"Here." He removes the money clip from his inside jacket pocket and peels off several hundreds.

"I don't want your money." Panic is growing inside me. I need to get away from him before I embarrass myself with tears or pleading.

"Don't be stubborn. Just take it." He ignores my protests and tucks the cash into the cleavage revealed by my tank top. "It's the least I can do. You'll need cab money at the very least."

"Thanks." Conflicting emotions expand in my chest. I'm ready to move forward with my life, but I know I'll never see him again. Now that the moment has arrived, the truth is even more painful than anticipated. I back away. Force a smile that I don't feel. "See ya."

"Right. See ya." He echoes my casual tone. I walk toward the terminal door. After a dozen heartbeats, the car door closes, and the motor revs. I resist the urge to glance over my shoulder. I can't. If I do, I'll run back to the limo and beg him to take me with him.

Outside the airport, I sit on the bench at the bus stop and stare into space through watery eyes. After the brightness of the Caribbean, the city seems dingy and beige. I try to formulate a plan. Once I find a cheap motel, I'll need a phone, some clothes, and a job. The money Nicky gave me won't go far. My bus pulls up to the curb. Right behind it is Nicky's limo. My heart gives an awkward lurch. He exits the car and strides toward me with the smoldering intensity I've come to adore. "Get in the car, Jones."

"What?"

"Just do it." He lowers his sunglasses, giving me a glimpse of his thick-lashed gray irises. "You're staying with me."

TWENTY-FIVE

Calliope

"It's perfect." The saleswoman circles me, adjusting the seams of the little black dress to her liking.

On the way to his apartment, Nicky insisted on visiting a few shops to pick up clothes. This is our third stop. He sits in a highbacked blue velvet chair in the fitting room, a glass of champagne in his left hand and a tray of caviar on the table at his right. The saleswoman bats her lashes at him. "Do you like it, Nicky?"

I don't want to know why he's on a first-name basis with all the women in these shops, but I can guess. His gaze crawls over my breasts, the cutouts exposing my waistline, and my bare thighs below the short hemline. The intense scrutiny heightens my embarrassment and creates a funny twinge between my legs. "It's okay. What do you think, Calliope?"

"I don't like it." I fidget, shifting to get away from the scratchy fabric. "It's too tight in the boobs."

“Hm…I see what you mean.” He leans back in the chair. “Bring us something else. Something dazzling.”

“I think I have just the thing.” The woman gestures to her assistant who wheels in a rack filled with more designs. “This just came in today.”

Nicky watches while I change into the new dress. The jersey knit is held together by studded leather belts. Cutouts reveal slivers of my skin. His lashes lower, hooding his eyes. “Now that’s more like it. You look good enough to eat.”

“It’s called a bondage dress.” The saleswoman brightens at his compliment, like he’s talking to her instead of me.

I spin slowly in front of the three-way mirror. The strategic placement of the leather straps lifts my breasts to impossible heights. Although it’s hard for me to admit, I look damn good. The heat in Nicky’s stare bolsters my confidence. “Tell me again why I need a cocktail dress?”

“Because we’re going out for dinner tonight, and you can’t wear Rourke’s shorts.” He extends a credit card to the saleswoman. “We’ll take it. Ring it up and take your time. We’re going to need a minute.”

“Absolutely. No hurry.” She rushes off, ecstatic over her commission.

The instant the door closes behind her, Nicky tugs me into his lap. Something hard and insistent prods my thigh. His delicious mouth hovers an inch away. “Let me help you out of this.” Before I can protest, his lips brush along mine, velvety and soft. I fall headlong into the kiss. After a long time, we part. I'm left breathless with an ache between my legs and fire in my veins. His widespread fingers on my back steady me. "Next, we're going to the lingerie store. I can't wait to see your new panties on my bedroom floor."

As much as I adore having his mouth and hands on me, I can't escape the nagging idea that sex is part of this deal. The thought sickens me. Before Valentina, I would have slept with him for this dress, but not now. Not when his respect means so much to me. I push on his shoulders to gain some space between us. "I appreciate all this. I really do, but it will take me ten years to pay you back for the dress, let alone lingerie."

He shifts my weight on his thighs. His palm slides lower on my back to cup my ass. The gesture is possessive and male and panty-melting. "I don't want you to pay me back. The clothes are a gift."

"No. I'm serious." I squirm, needing to get away from his touch, but he tightens his grip on my bottom. The walls of my pussy clench. "I don't want money to be a thing between us. I'd always feel like I owe you." Tears burn in my throat. "I had enough of that with Cash." He'd always held my debts over my head, using it as leverage to make me do things I never wanted to do.

Nicky slides his nose along mine then rests his forehead on my temple. "Can't a guy buy nice things for his girlfriend?" My heart skips a beat. I hold my breath, thinking I imagined the question. He nuzzles my ear. "Come home with me, Jones. Be my girlfriend."

My breath escapes with a whoosh. I curl my fingers into the fabric of his suit, loving the smell of his cologne and the heat of his body. This can't be happening, can it? His wicked smile confirms the truth. This is real. This is my life. "I suppose we can work something out."

"Great." He gently nudges me to my feet and gives my ass a smack. "Let's get out of here. I was going to have my way with you in here, but I'm going to need a bed for what I have in mind."

Later that evening, we're at Swerve, Nicky's upscale Manhattan restaurant. From our seats, we have an unparalleled view of New York City, the towering skyscrapers, and the Hudson River. The table linens are silk, the chairs are brocaded velvet, and the surfaces are clad in slate and polished wood. Gazing around the dining room, I spot familiar faces—celebrities, politicians, and rock stars. Even though I'm wearing a five thousand-dollar gown, I feel out of place. On the outside, I've been coiffed and styled to perfection. Inside, I'm still the former stripper and prostitute from Indiana.

The waiter pauses next to our table, a worried frown clouding his face. "Is the champagne to your liking, sir? Would you like anything else?"

"We're fine. Nothing more this evening." Nicky's attention returns to me. His gaze rakes over me, bringing the sting of blood to my breasts. "You look beautiful. That dress is amazing. The bondage look is good for you. Who's your stylist?" A mischievous grin reaches his eyes, giving them depth and sparkle.

"You are." I smile back, despite my insecurities about my body and past life. "Thank you so much."

"You're welcome." The brutal beauty of his face is still there, but I see past the storm in his eyes and the perfection of his chiseled features to the man inside. He reaches across the table to take my hand in his. The pad of his thumb traces circles on the underside of my wrist, sending a shiver of need up my back. "You know, I was thinking. You could come to work for Roman and me. Your skills could come in handy." His eyebrow lifts. Opportunity and optimism shine in his gaze.

"What kind of skills?" Every caress of his thumb reminds me that I'm a lucky girl. Sitting in this restaurant with him is beyond thrilling. A kernel of hope takes root in my soul. Maybe this will work.

"You're resourceful, sneaky, and have sticky fingers. Something men in our line of work covet." He taps a fingertip on the back of my hand. "I'm offering you a job, Jones."

"Really?" I bite my lower lip, afraid to get excited. Too many times in the past, my dreams have been crushed.

"Yes. Really." His tongue slides over his lower lip while his gaze remains glued to my mouth. "We talked about it earlier. It was his idea, actually." He leans back in the chair. "We'll pay you a decent salary, of course. And you'll have to sign an intense NDA."

"I'd like that." My smile broadens until the muscles in my cheeks ache. A real job. Making real money. A future. "I can get an apartment."

"I think you should live with me." He lifts my hand and kisses my fingertips. "I've gotten used to having you around."

The moment is shattered by a deep voice. A familiar voice. One I've forgotten in the heat of the day's events. "Calliope? I thought that was you."

"Cash?" Sweat breaks out on my palms. I drag my hand from Nicky's grasp, into my lap, and clench my fingers into a fist. The past comes crashing into my bright, shiny future. "What are you doing here?"

"Having dinner." As always, a black suit showcases his blond hair, broad shoulders, and narrow hips. His gaze sweeps over my expensive dress. "I could ask the same of you."

"We haven't met. I'm Nicky Tarnovsky, the owner of this establishment." Nicky folds his napkin. Tosses it into his plate. He stands to his full height, staring Cash in the eyes. There's no mistaking the clench of his jaw.

"Cash Delacorte." Cash stares back at Nicky with equal animosity. It's like watching two lions circle a tasty lamb. "I'm familiar with your work, Mr. Tarnovsky. We run in similar circles. It's an honor to meet you." He smooths a hand over his tie, uncertainty clouding his strong features. I have to admit, it's amusing to see him off balance.

"I can't say the same for you." Nicky's lips turn down in a sneer. "You're interrupting our dinner. Did you want something?" His features sharpen into the cold, brutal man who stalked me at the bar.

Two security men approach. Nicky holds them at bay with a flick of his fingers. The rapid drum of my heart slows. I'm safe here. Nicky won't let anything happen to me. Not now. Not ever. A sense of calm chases away the fear.

"You owe me," Cash says through clenched teeth, shifting his gaze to meet mine. "I want my money back."

"I don't owe you shit." The vehemence in my voice surprises all of us. "You did nothing but take from me. My dignity, my self-respect, my love." Anger flickers in his gold eyes. I don't care about his feelings anymore. Despite his efforts, I'm free from his control. "That's all the repayment you'll ever get."

After a nod of approval at my declaration, Nicky takes a step toward Cash. "You heard her. If you ever so much as look in her direction again, I'll have you cut into so many pieces, no one will be able to put your corpse back together again. Now, I suggestion you leave and never come back."

TWENTY-SIX

Calliope

With a sigh of satisfaction, I step back from the dining room to survey my work. Six place settings of Nicky's fine china and an exotic centerpiece of tulips grace the table. Soft jazz music floats from the hidden speakers. It's our first dinner party as a couple and our six-month anniversary. Everything needs to be perfect.

"Jones?" Nicky shouts at me from the depths of the penthouse. "Calliope?"

"What?" I hustle down the hallway to our shared closet. He's staring at the pile of dirty clothes on top of the hamper. "Oh. Sorry." I lift the lid and chuck them inside. "I got distracted."

"How hard is it to put them inside the hamper?" A furrow mars his forehead. "It's right *there*."

"I know. I know." I balance on tiptoe to plant a kiss on his cheek.

"You've been saying that for months." With a

disgusted grunt, he heads for the master bathroom to shave. He's wearing black boxer briefs and nothing else. The sight of his naked torso stirs a sense of wonderment. This male god is my boyfriend. *Mine.*

"I'll do better." I steal up behind him and wrap my arms around his waist. His bare skin is warm and still damp from his recent shower. I rest my cheek on his back. "Has anyone ever told you that you're an obsessive neat freak?"

"Has anyone told you that you're a slob?"

"All the time. You tell me every day."

Our eyes meet in the mirror. A smile replaces his scowl. He drops the razor and turns to embrace me. I bury my nose in the notch of his collarbone. This is my safe place. My haven. I treasure moments like these, when it's just the two of us doing mundane things. His lips skim over the top of my head. "I love having your dirty clothes on top of my hamper."

"And I love putting them there." A chuckle rumbles through him. I press a kiss to his chest.

"Do we have time for a quickie?" His hands wander lower on my back. The steely length of his erection presses into my stomach. "Pretty please?"

"No. They'll be here in fifteen minutes. You better get a move on." I try unsuccessfully to disentangle myself from his embrace. He digs his fingers into my bottom and peppers kisses along my throat. I push on his chest. "Stop. You're going to mess up my hair."

With a mischievous smirk, he lifts a handful of

tresses to his nose and sniffs. "Who cares? I like it messy."

"I care. It's not every day that a billionaire and a king come to my house for dinner." I wriggle out of his grasp, putting a few feet of distance between us. "Now, hurry up."

"You're no fun." With a manly pout, he returns to the business of shaving.

"Oh, really? Just wait until our guests leave. I'm going to rock your world." I pause in the doorway to lift the hem of my dress, revealing the sassy red bow at the top of my tiny thong.

The razor slips from his fingers and clatters into the sink. He swallows hard enough to make his Adam's apple bob. "I'm going to hold you to that."

In exactly fifteen minutes, the doorman buzzes to let us know our guests are on their way up. My stomach does a nervous flip. I haven't seen these people since our time together on Roman's yacht. Nicky notices my anxiety and pulls me into the crook of his shoulder. "Easy now."

"I hope everything is okay." I've never thrown a dinner party before. And never for some of the richest people in the world. "Maybe this was a mistake."

"It will be fine. Trust me." He tilts my face up to his and plants the tenderest of kisses on my mouth. The confidence in his gray eyes steadies my nerves. "Besides, who gives a fuck what they think? Not me."

"Well, I do. They're your friends, and I want them to

like me." After our rocky start, I'm eager to make a good impression.

Before our guests arrive, I take one last look around the penthouse. I've added feminine touches to the masculine tones of his décor here and there, and it feels like home. Nicky heads toward the door. He turns and flashes his mischievous grin. My heart skips a beat, the same way it does every time I look at him. Our relationship isn't perfect, but it's the best thing in my life. In such a short time, we've been through so much. He started out as my kidnapper, but what he really stole was my heart.

***

I hope you enjoyed the story. If you did, please consider leaving a review. For more about Calliope's little sister and Cash Delacorte, keep an eye out for the ABSOLUTE POWER DUET, coming in 2020. In the meantime, please enjoy this excerpt of LIES WE TELL, available everywhere in March 2020.

Through the peephole of my front door, I saw the broad width of Owen Henry's chest and the sharp, chiseled lines of his jaw. I leaned against the door, my heart banging into my ribs, and weighed my options. If I opened the door, it would be like unlocking the vault containing all of my dirty, sordid secrets. If I ignored the man outside, he might go away, but I couldn't ignore how memories of him had made me touch myself in the dark, quiet hours of the night for the past eighteen years.

"Hello?" The door vibrated under his second, harsher knock. I jumped back. His voice was deeper than I remembered, like he'd just tumbled out of bed after a sleepless night. "Ms. Valentine?"

I rested my forehead on the door and placed a palm on the barrier between us. "Crap," I hated myself for cowering in the foyer, hated him for knocking on my door.

This time, the doorbell rang. "Ms. Valentine? Hello?" The words came from an unfamiliar voice. I peered through the peephole and blinked. A stocky, middle-aged man stood in the weak light of daybreak. My nightmare/fantasy guy was nowhere in sight. Had I imagined him? Maybe it had only been someone who looked like Owen. I opened the door an inch and peered at the man's ruddy face and pleasant smile. His silver hair and bushy eyebrows reminded me of Santa Claus.

"Hi. I'm George Sherman, your general contractor. We spoke on the phone yesterday." He scanned my wet hair, bathrobe, and bare legs. An anxious frown creased his forehead. "I'm a little early, but we did say seven-thirty, right?"

"Yes, we did, and please call me Stella." Behind him, lavender and pink light stretched across the horizon. If I hadn't been so rattled, I'd have run for my camera to capture the skyscape. Instead, I skimmed the yard and driveway, trying not to look panicked, searching for signs of Owen. Maybe lack of sleep had made me hallucinate. I touched the towel on my head. "Sorry. The hot water stopped in the middle of my shower." If I'd been tired before, the icy water had left me in a state of invigorated exhaustion. "Let me run upstairs and change. Why don't you come in?"

"That's okay. I don't want to get your floors dirty." His gaze dropped to his work boots, dusty from the trek across the overgrown yard. I followed his glance then studied the worn floor. If my estimate was correct, it hadn't seen a mop in over a decade. He tapped a pen on his clipboard. "I'll get my crew started on the roof, like we talked about. You and I can do a walk-through of the house when you're ready. And I'll have one of the boys take a look at your water heater. Does that sound okay?"

"Perfect. I'm eager to get moving on this." One of my foster parents, in a strange twist, had left the house to me in his will. In my memories, this place had been in much better condition. After a lifetime of wandering, this house offered the opportunity to put down roots. I wasn't sure, however, that I could overlook the past, and if *he* was here—Owen—my doubts doubled.

"Call me Dad. Everyone does." George's weathered skin crinkled around his eyes. He turned and bellowed to the crew in the driveway, "Alright, boys. Let's get this party started."

Owen rounded the corner of the house. I sucked my lower lip between my teeth and bit down hard. He was the kind of guy who made a woman look twice. Scruffy stubble on his square jaw, brown hair streaked by the sun, and biceps worthy of a prizefighter. I gaped, wondering if the world had shifted into some kind of alternate universe. My body shook like a leaf in the wind.

The memory of Owen's lips gliding over my bare breasts blasted through my head. I crossed my arms over my chest to hide the sting of arousal in my nipples. The wind stilled, leaving the air thick and stagnant. Even the birds, who'd been twittering, halted their morning song. Owen's eyes met mine. The color drained from his sunburned face. His wide chest lifted with a sharp intake of breath. Yep, he was definitely my ex-boyfriend. The murderer. And he was as shocked to see me as I was to see him.

"Shit," I muttered. Why, why, why? Why now? Why here? Before I'd accepted the inheritance, I'd done a Google search on his whereabouts. When I'd come up with nothing, I'd assumed he'd moved away. I shook my head at my gullibility. His family still lived here. This was his home. Of course, he hadn't left.

"Are you okay? Ms. Valentine?" Dad gripped my elbow as the world spun. "Stella?"

"Yes. I just—I need to sit down for a minute." No matter how hard I tried, I couldn't draw in a full breath. My lungs burned from lack of oxygen.

"Let me help you." The warm concern in Dad's voice eased a bit of my anxiety. He led me to the folding chair in the living room, my only piece of furniture, and held my arm while I eased into the seat. "Can I get you anything? Some water?"

"What's going on?" The voice of Michael, my sort-of-kind-of-but-not-really boyfriend, floated up the front steps. The storm door banged shut behind him. Dad would have to fix that too. "What happened?"

"I think I'm having a panic attack. Let me sit for a second. I'll be fine." The room continued to swim, the colors melting into a blurred mess. Michael kneeled at my side, dropping two takeout bags at my feet. The minute his hand found mine, my heartbeat steadied. He had that kind of effect on people, an innate strength that clung to men in positions of power, men like him. "What are you doing here?"

"I brought breakfast. A housewarming gift." The paper bag rustled as he dug inside and withdrew an orange juice. "Here. Drink, sweetie." Over the rim of the bottle, my eyes met his brown ones. Short, bristly black lashes surrounded his chocolate irises, giving his angular features a deceptively sweet air. The squeeze of his hand on my knee corralled my attention. "Better?"

"Yes. Better." I nodded and gave him a sheepish smile, but my stomach churned with concern. Somewhere, outside, Owen awaited. How was I going to face him? Or answer the questions Michael would ask when he learned of our connection?

"Don't scare me like that. Maybe next time you'll listen to me when I say you should eat regular meals."

"Probably not." As always, he was right. I hadn't eaten since leaving Cleveland yesterday—too nervous about my new home, about returning to Indiana, about the ghosts of my past, to think of mundane things like food. Arguing with Michael did no good. As the county's district attorney and a potential senate candidate, he took pride in winning every debate, whether personal or professional.

"Of course, what was I thinking? Stella Valentine doesn't listen to anyone." Despite his rebuke, a smile brightened his handsome face. With gentle fingertips, he brushed back the hair from my forehead. "Stubborn mule."

"You worry too much." I had to look away from his trusting gaze, afraid he'd see the darkness lurking in my soul, the secrets threatening to spill out.

"You don't worry enough, in my opinion." He chucked me under the chin, stood, and held out a hand to Dad. "You must be the contractor. I'm Michael Ludlow."

"I know who you are, Mr. Ludlow. It's an honor to meet you, sir. I voted for you in the last election." They shook hands. "You can call me Dad."

"Thanks for the support. I appreciate it." Michael studied him for a beat. "Stella tells me you come highly recommended. I trust you'll take care of her."

"Absolutely," Dad said.

"If you don't mind, I'd like to see your plans and the bid." Michael straightened the knot in his tie, using his best business stare. Dad glanced in my direction for permission.

"I mind," I said, finding my strength and voice at the

same time. "Stop worrying. I've got everything under control."

"Stubborn *and* independent." Michael winked at Dad. "You'd better watch out for this one."

"There's a lot to be said for a woman who knows her mind," Dad replied quietly. His statement made me like him even more. "And, if it eases your worries, she's an excellent negotiator. I probably won't make a dime on this project." His eyes crinkled again. I gave him a grateful nod. "If you're good, Stella, I'll get to work."

"Thank you." Although my words were confident, my smile wavered. How would I make it through these renovations with Owen on his crew? Maybe I should cancel the whole thing and look for another contractor. I dismissed the idea as overly dramatic and straightened my backbone.

As soon as the door closed behind Dad, Michael grabbed my elbow and gave me a gentle push toward the stairs. "Are you crazy? Opening the door in your bathrobe? In front of all those men?"

"Well, someone had to do it." Sometimes, like now, his ultra-conservativism got on my nerves. We were miles apart in every way—upbringing, social class, personalities—but because he made me feel safe, I chose to overlook our differences. To avoid an argument, I changed the subject. "So why are you really here? I'm not exactly on your way to work."

"I'm going to New York on personal business. I wanted to see you before I left. Is that okay?"

Butterflies skittered in my stomach. I pulled back to

search his face. We'd been living in different states, commuting on weekends, since we'd met three months ago. With my hectic schedule as a freelance photographer and his job as county prosecutor, we barely saw each other. When Stan had willed his house to me, it had given me the opportunity to move closer to Michael. Maybe I'd jumped the gun, but I really liked him and wanted this to work.

Following a tender kiss, he chucked me beneath the chin. "Discussion over. Now, run upstairs and put on some clothes. Then you can give me a tour of your new money pit."

"Okay." My friends in Cleveland thought I was crazy to uproot my life and move to Indiana after such a short relationship, but they didn't know Michael the way I did. He was smart and handsome and successful, everything I'd ever wanted in a man, and he truly cared about me.

From a suitcase on the floor, I drew out a pair of slouchy jeans and a T-shirt and got dressed. I was used living on the road, roughing it. The dented plaster and peeling ceilings didn't bother me. Overhead, footsteps thumped across the roof. Thoughts of Michael evaporated. Through the window, I watched the workers unload bags of shingles onto the driveway. The rumble of rough voices and male laughter floated on a steamy breeze.

I closed my eyes and conjured the memory of a face that had haunted my dreams since my sophomore year in high school. Wide hazel eyes with lashes longer than mine. A square jaw peppered with stubble and a mouth meant for kisses—long, slow, panty-melting kisses. Even though eighteen years had passed, not a day went by that I didn't think of Owen Henry, the way I'd loved him, or the horrible thing he'd done because of me.

"I can't work here." The emphatic words floated up from the driveway. My eyes flew open. Owen stood next to the truck, tool belt and car keys in hand. I couldn't see his face, but his shoulders tensed. "I'm sorry, Dad. It's just not possible."

Dad said something too soft for my ears to catch across the distance, but Owen's posture relaxed. After a few seconds, he nodded and glanced up at me. I shrank back, hiding behind the curtain. The memories I'd locked away flooded into my head, insistent and unrelenting. Apparently, a leaky roof and faulty plumbing were the least of my problems.

Also by Jeana E. Mann

RICH, ROYAL AND RUTHLESS COLLECTION

(In reading order)

THE EXILED PRINCE TRILOGY

The Exiled Prince

The Dirty Princess

The War King

THE REBEL QUEEN DUET

The Royal Arrangement

The Rebel Queen

(Standalone)

The Ruthless Knight

PRETTY BROKEN SERIES

(In reading order)

Pretty Broken Girl

Pretty Filthy Lies

Pretty Dirty Secrets

Pretty Wild Thing

Pretty Broken Promises

Pretty Broken Dreams

Pretty Broken Baby

Pretty Broken Hearts

Pretty Broken Bastard

FELONY ROMANCE SERIES

(In reading order)

Intoxicated

Unexpected

Vindicated

Impulsive

Drift

Committed

STANDALONES

Lies We Tell

Dirty Work

SHORT STORIES

<u>Everything</u>

<u>Linger</u>

Before You Go

DID YOU ENJOY READING THIS BOOK?

Please, please consider leaving a review. Your review can mean the difference between success and failure for a struggling author.

- **Lend it.**
- **Recommend it.**
- **Review it.**

HELP AN AUTHOR — LEAVE A REVIEW!

About the Author

Jeana is a *USA Today* and *Publishers Weekly* bestselling author from Indiana. She gave up a career in the corporate world to write about sexy billionaires and alpha bad boys. With over twenty books, three series, and many awards beneath her belt, she's never regretted her choice to live out her dream. She's a free spirit, a wanderer at heart, and loves animals with a passion. When she's not tripping over random objects, you'll find her walking in the sunshine with her rambunctious dogs and dreaming about true love. Subscribe to Jeana's newsletter and get the inside scoop on new and upcoming releases, giveaways, and much more! CLICK HERE

TEXT ALERTS -

text the word "Jeana" without quotation marks to 21000 and get new release alerts straight to your phone.

Cover design by Jena Brignola

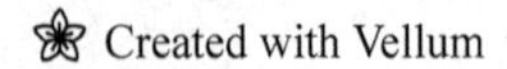

CPSIA information can be obtained
at www.ICGtesting.com
Printed in the USA
LVHW082351180220
647425LV00015B/507